THE SHEPHERD'S PIPE AND
OTHER STORIES

THE
SHEPHERD'S PIPE

AND OTHER STORIES

By

ARTHUR SCHNITZLER

Authorized Translation from the German
By
O. F. THEIS

Fredonia Books
Amsterdam, The Netherlands

The Shepherd's Pipe and Other Stories

by
Arthur Schnitzler

ISBN: 1-58963-994-4

Fredonia Books
Amsterdam, The Netherlands
http://www.fredoniabooks.com

CONTENTS

CONTENTS

INTRODUCTION

The Austrian writers who center around Vienna are different from the German writers of the North. They are not as hard, not as serious. They have a lighter touch and their sense of form is more highly developed. There is also in most of them an undercurrent of weariness, as though they belonged to a civilization which has lost its illusions and is slowly disintegrating. They often make one think of the last days of the *ancien régime* in France. There is something of the bloom and grace and artifice which make Fragonard, Boucher, and Watteau so appealing, but there is also something far more profound. They are men of the present time who have looked deeply into this modern world. As a generalization this applies to men like Hugo von Hofmannsthal, Peter Altenberg, Richard von Beer-Hofmann, Hermann Bahr, and many lesser men, but particularly to Arthur Schnitzler, who is the greatest of them all.

Schnitzler's art is not for those who demand
the emphatic gesture or the violence and
melodrama of elemental emotion. His types
are, almost without exception, of the world of
the well-to-do, of the complex, of the intelli-
gent, the people who are self-aware, but not
self-conscious. He is too wise to be dogmatic,
not naïve enough to become heroic in the conventional sense. He knows the immense
human capacity for self-deception, and remem-
bers how to smile at it without bitterness,
though often with a tear glistening in the
corner of his eye. Readers, however, with a
speculative curiosity about the workings of the
human mind, who care "for art in life as well
as life in art," will find his work of infinite
interest. It penetrates deep into the obscure
and intangible motives that influence or domi-
nate human relations.

Hermann Bahr once said of him: "We love
him because his art always wears gloves, never
makes the slightest obeisance to the mob, and
because the old Roman's *odi profanum vulgus
et arceo* might stand as a luminous motto over
each of his works."

This, however, must not be interpreted in
the sense that Schnitzler's art is snobbish or

has any of the chill of the Parnassians. It means that he never loses himself in those morals which are so often only the handed-down prejudices of the unthinking. Again and again the phrase, "Let us remember the essential," occurs in his works. Yet he knows, too, the power of the old and worn-out ideas and ideals that lurk in some forgotten corner of our intelligence; knows that it takes only a breath out of this childish world which all of us so despise with our heads to have the ancient goblins become alive and potent for evil again. This is often the theme of his drama.

A strange shuttle slips to and fro in Schnitzler's work, weaving invisible threads and associations that join lives for a time, only to have Fate come with her shears to clip them apart again. There may be a gay insouciance on the surface, but it is only a mask to hide the disillusioned hearts that are weary unto death. Life is a solitary passage through a twilight autumn landscape over which broods mystery. Who really knows another, and who really cares? "It is probably well we don't," answers one of the characters in the *Lonely Way*, "for otherwise we would all go mad with pity, fear, or disgust."

Somewhere Anatole France has said: "For those who understand it properly, the world has but two faces. Look all over the world, nature will show you nothing but love and death. It is for this reason that it smiles on man, and that its smile is sometimes so sad." Something like this is Schnitzler's point of view too, but love sometimes gives moments that simulate eternity. Even so, it is a two-edged sword, that cuts keenly through the romantic illusions with which poets and dreamers have endowed it.

Death alone he always treats reverently, almost with awe. He is a physician, and must often have seen it at close range. He sees in it the great aim and end-all of human existence. He knows its mystery; he regards the dread of it as humanity's most natural and normal emotion. When he deals with death it is as a simple function of life. There is none of the theatrical artifice of Maeterlinck's *Intruder*, none of the neurosis of D'Annunzio's *Triumph of Death*.

Things are not what they seem, and seem not what they are. Illusion and reality, truth and untruth, play and earnest, are all an inextricable pattern. Love and death alone give it form; life is a game forever in flux.

> "All that we on earth pursue is but a game,
> It matters not how great or deep it seem.
> One plays the game with mercenary hordes,
> Another plays with superstitious mobs.
> Some one, perhaps, with suns and stars somewhere—
> With human souls play I. And what purport
> There may be, he only finds who searches deep.
> Dream and waking into each other flow,
> Truth and falsity—nowhere certainty.
> Of others we know naught, naught of ourselves;
> We always play, he who knows it is wise."

Thus Paracelsus speaks in the play of that name, and how like this is to an answer which that other great skeptic of the present day, Anatole France, once made when asked why he actively participated in political strife: "One may not be able to do; but one may play. The struggle of the political parties is for me a titanic game of chess. But are not all the deeds of mankind games? The gods play with us—in that lies our tragedy; let us, then, play with the gods—it may be that then our tragedies will end in an idyl. He who has lost faith in everything derives the innocent ease and delight of divine games from everything.

Oh, how sweet it is to rest upon the pillow of doubt!"

These are merely a few hints of the richness that lies in Schnitzler's work. Critics have pointed to flaws. They say there is too much uniformity of mood and type, too much resignation and acceptance, too little will. Be that as it may, the reader must accept him as he is. And why not? There are not many who are writing to-day whose play of wit is as light, whose mind is as graceful and agile, whose skepticism has in it so little of cruelty, whose laughter is as gentle and whose tears as sincere, and whose wisdom is as deep or whose tolerance is as universal.

Biographical details in regard to Schnitzler are meagre. He was born May 15, 1862, the son of a physician. He himself studied medicine. In addition to his profession he early devoted himself to literature, and a long series of plays, stories, and novels, both long and short, have come from his pen. From his earliest work to his last he has never faltered; his literary ideal has always been high.

The stories in the present volume have not appeared in English before. They belong to his second period, when he had already reached full maturity. The title story is one of Schnitzler's most characteristic creations. It is told with the simplicity of an ancient legend. The heroine's husband, a sage, tells her she is free, and is to obey whatever impulse may come to her. He will wait for her until she returns, and receive her without a word of reproach. A shepherd's pipe lures her away, and with him she wanders through the world. Later she falls in with a master of men, an industrialist who thinks he is making over the world, but partly through her fault his workingmen revolt, and she is swept into the midst of a horde of camp-followers. She is rescued by a hero, whose bride and companion she becomes and to whom she bears a son. After his death on the battlefield, she turns into the frivolous mistress of a prince. Finally she comes home again to her husband who meets her with the words: "Neither question nor reproach shall ever torment you. Here you will find safety; without, lurk danger and death." But more than all else she fears the stony grimace of his wisdom, and disappears forever into the unknown. It is a wonderful symbol of woman, and an almost uncanny prophecy of the Europe that has come as the result of the war.

The other stories were selected for this volume by Doctor Schnitzler himself. In all three of the stories there have been almost insurmountable difficulties of translation. They are filled with nuances and a peculiar mellow prose rhythm which it is very difficult to convey in English. It is almost as though one were to try to turn the later Henry James into a foreign language. However, the translator hopes that he has acquitted himself of his task sufficiently well to give the English reader some idea of Schnitzler's peculiar quality.

O. F. T.

THE SHEPHERD'S PIPE

THE SHEPHERD'S PIPE

A YOUNG man of well-to-do family, who as a youth had idled about considerably among people, both in the city and the country, and who as amateur had pursued all sorts of sciences and arts, in his maturer years undertook a journey into distant lands and did not return to his native country until his hair was already turning gray. In a retired part of the country, at a forest's edge, he built himself a house which looked out on the wide plain, and took to wife the gentle, only recently orphaned daughter of a husbandman. His parents and relatives had long been dead; he no longer felt drawn to the friends of former days, to win new ones did not tempt him much. It was a region over which a clear blue sky hung almost perpetually, and so he gave himself to the study of the courses of the stars, a science to which he was especially devoted.

Once on a sultry night, when as usual Erasmus had been indulging in his tower in his occupation, vapors arose from the damp meadows and gradually obscured every view toward the celestial distances. Erasmus descended the stairs. Earlier than was his wont on clear nights, he entered the conjugal chamber, where he found his wife already asleep. Without waking her, he let his eyes rest upon her for a long time. Though her lids remained closed and her lineaments without motion, he watched her with tense, constantly growing attention, as if in this hour he had to explore the activity of the thoughts which hitherto had remained hidden from him behind this smooth, peaceful forehead. At last he extinguished the light, and sat down in an armchair at the foot of the bed. In the silence of the night he abandoned himself to a wholly unaccustomed musing concerning the being with whom for three years he had been united in calm, untroubled wedlock; and to-day for the first time she seemed like some one who was wholly a stranger to him.

It was only when the tall window began to gleam under the rising light of early dawn that he rose. He then waited patiently until under his glance Dionysia took a deep breath, stretched, opened her eyes, and greeted him with a serene good-morning smile. When she saw him standing in such immobile seriousness at the foot of the bed, she asked in surprise, and at first in a jesting tone:

"What has happened to you, my Erasmus? Couldn't you find your way about in the skies to-night? Were there too many clouds? Or was there some star that escaped into infinity, so that even with your magnificent new telescope you couldn't bring it back?"

Erasmus remained silent.

Dionysia raised herself up a little, looked searchingly at her husband, and went on asking:

"Why do you not answer? Has something evil happened to you? Are you feeling ill? Or have I, perhaps, without knowing it, given offence? That is what I suppose I must assume. Because were it any other hurt I myself would be here to heal and comfort you, and you would not withhold your answer so long."

Now at last Erasmus determined to speak.

"From you, Dionysia," he began, "it is impossible this time to receive either healing or comfort; my abstracted manner comes from this, that for many long hours I have thought concerning you, and likewise became conscious that until to-night I had never before done this."

Dionysia rested on her pillows and smiled.

"And do you now know differently, or better than before, that you have a tender, faithful, and happy wife, as your own?"

"It is quite possible," replied Erasmus sombrely, "that you are all this. Only the worst is I cannot know it and you can know it as little as I."

"What are you saying? Whence come such doubts all of a sudden?"

"I will tell you, Dionysia. Never was an opportunity given to me really to know you— nor to you to know yourself. For you used to live quietly under the shelter of the paternal roof and now at my side. What title have you, or what right have I, to assume that your tenderness signifies love, your constancy faithfulness, the equanimity of your soul happiness, and that they would stand the test in the stress and storm of an intenser life?"

Now Dionysia nodded as if comforted. "Do you really believe," she asked, "that hitherto temptations have never assailed me? Did I keep hidden from you that before you desired my hand other men sued for it, younger men—

yes, and even wiser men than you? And without any possibility of anticipating your coming, my dear Erasmus, I sent all of them away without hesitation. And even in the present days, when wanderers stray past the hedge-row of our garden, I often see glowing dangerous questions and desires in their young eyes. To not one of them has my glance ever given an answer. And even the foreign scientists, who hold converse with you concerning the comets of coming centuries, seldom neglect an opportunity to hint by a play of the eyes and by smiles that my favor would be more precious to them than all knowledge of sun, moon, and stars. Have I ever shown to any one of these a courtesy other than is seemly to guests that eat at our table?"

Mockingly Erasmus replied:

"Surely, Dionysia, you do not imagine that with these words you are telling me something new, for I know men. But even if your conduct always has been beyond reproach, do I therefore know, and do you yourself know, Dionysia, whether your unapproachableness represents your real inner conviction? Have you not withstood every appeal, and believe yourself determined to withstand them also in the

future, because up to the present the thought
has never come to you that circumstances
might be different; or because secretly you are
afraid you might lose the accustomed ease of
existence, should you ever try to set yourself
above the laws of conventional marriage?"

"I do not understand," said Dionysia in
alarm, "what you mean by all this. I haven't
the slightest desire to attempt anything like
that; and I can assure you that I feel perfectly
contented and happy in my present state."

"I do not doubt this, Dionysia. But don't
you understand yet, that to me this means
nothing any longer, can mean nothing, since
in the silent hour of the night I had the vision
that the deepest secret of your soul may lie still
hidden and unawakened in you? To find
again the peace which otherwise is lost to me
forever, it is imperative that this secret be
brought to the light of day; and therefore,
Dionysia, I have determined to set you free."

"To set me free?" Dionysia repeated helplessly, with wide-open eyes.

Without hesitation, Erasmus continued:
"Listen to me, Dionysia, and try to understand
me. From this moment on I give up all rights
to you, which hitherto belonged to me: the

right to warn you, to restrain you, to punish you. Indeed, I rather demand that you follow without hesitation every impulse of curiosity that stirs in you, every desire that calls you. And at the same time, Dionysia, I make a vow unto you. You may go from here whither you will, with whomever you will—when you will, whether you return home to-day or in ten years—whether as queen or beggar-woman, whether untouched or as a harlot—you will find always your chamber, your bed, your gown, waiting for you in this house, just as you left them. And from me who will continue to abide here, but who will not be waiting for you, you need fear through all the future neither reproach nor even a question."

Dionysia stretched out in the bed, her hands clasped over her head, and asked: "Do you mean this that you are saying seriously or in jest?"

"I mean it so seriously, Dionysia, that nothing in the world, neither prayer nor supplication, could move me to withdraw the words I have just spoken. Please understand me, and take what I have said in its largest significance. Dionysia, you are free."

And he turned from her as if to leave.

It was then that Dionysia threw off the coverlet, ran to the window and tore it open; had Erasmus not hastened to her side she would have lain crushed far below in a second.

"Unhappy woman!" he cried, holding her trembling in his arms; "what were you about to do?"

"End a life which is without meaning to me, since I have lost your confidence."

Erasmus' lips touched the forehead of his wife; she seemed to be losing consciousness in his arms, and he took a deep breath.

Suddenly melodious sounds became disengaged from the silence of the valley which lay gray in the dawn. Dionysia opened her eyes, and listened; her expression, which had been relaxed in despairing weariness, assumed new life. Erasmus noticed it, and immediately released Dionysia from his embrace.

"Do you recognize the sound that is rising to us?" he asked. "They are the notes of a shepherd's pipe. And see, without wishing to confess it to yourself and without being really quite aware of it, curiosity stirs in you, who a moment ago sought death, to discover whose lips touch the pipe from which these sounds rise. So it is time for you, Dionysia, to understand, what before, perhaps, you could not understand: that you are free. Follow this first call which comes to you—and every other which still may come, just as this one did. Go your way, Dionysia, to fulfill your destiny, to be wholly yourself."

With sorrowful astonishment Dionysia turned her glance toward her husband.

"Go your way," repeated Erasmus more decisively than before. "This is my last command to you. Perhaps, the note of this pipe is the only temptation to which you are destined to succumb; perhaps, it is only the first of a few or of many. Perhaps, another will call you back to this house within the next hour; perhaps, you will reappear in years; perhaps, never. But one thing remember always: Whenever you return, and burdened with whatever memories—bed, gown, and homestead are waiting for you. There will be neither question nor reproach to hurt you, and I myself shall receive you no otherwise than on the evening when as my young wife you passed across this threshold. And now, Dionysia, farewell."

With these words and with a last look he turned, went to the door, closed it behind him and wandered slowly up the stairs to the chamber in his tower. He had not stood long at the little peer-window with eyes turned toward the valley when he saw his wife hastening across the meadow with a curiously wing-like stride which he had never known in her; she was going toward the nearby forest from whose shadows the song of the pipe floated out to meet her. Soon she disappeared beneath the trees, and in the next minute Erasmus heard the pipe grow silent.

II

The young shepherd who, lying under a tree, had blinked up into the blue of the heavens through the leaves, let his pipe sink from his lips when he heard a rustling noise close by. He was not a little surprised, when he saw a young woman in a white flowing nightgown, standing barefooted in the moss before him.

"What do you want?" he asked. "Why do you look so angrily at me? Is it, perhaps, forbidden to blow a pipe here at this early hour? Did I wake you from your morning slumbers? Let me tell you, that I am accustomed to rise with the sun, and that I blow whenever I please. And this I shall continue, I give you my word."

With these words the shepherd shook his head so that his curls scattered about; he stretched out again at full length, blinked toward the sky, and put his pipe to his mouth.

"Who are you?" asked Dionysia, deeply moved.

Angrily the youth put his pipe aside and replied:

"I should think it wouldn't be difficult to see that I am a shepherd." And he continued piping.

"Where is your flock?" asked Dionysia.

"Don't you see something white gleam among the tree trunks over there? In the meadow my sheep are grazing. But I would advise you not to go close to them, for they are timid and scatter to all quarters of the wind, when they scent strangers near by." And again he was about to put his pipe to his lips.

"How do you happen to come into this region?" asked Dionysia. "I do not know you."

Now the youth leaped up and replied angrily:

"I go with my flock through all the land. One day I am here, the second there, the third elsewhere, and so all manner of things have already happened to me, but never before has it

happened to me that, at the crack of dawn,
ladies stand in front of me in the moss in their
nightgown, and ask me about things which are
no concern of theirs, just when I wish to blow
my pipe and blink at the young sun."

He measured Dionysia contemptuously from
head to foot; set his pipe to his mouth, and
walked away, still playing, toward the shimmering meadow. Then Dionysia felt ashamed
of her bare feet and her nightgown, and she
turned to go back to the house. But as the
notes sounded further and further away, the
thought flashed in her mind: Impudent boy.
I would like to break his pipe. And it occurred
to her that she had not the right to return
home, until she had followed the impulse, and
hurriedly she pursued the notes of the pipe
through the forest. Twigs beat against her
forehead, leaves remained clinging to her
loosened hair, and twisted roots twined around
her feet. But she paid no attention to this;
with her delicate fingers she broke the twigs
that obstructed her passage, struggled out of
the tangle on the ground, and shook the leaves
from her hair.

When she emerged from the forest, the green
meadow with blue, red, and white flowers

sloped down before her, and on the further side
where the forest began again stood the shepherd in the midst of his gleaming animals, and
his curls shone in the sunlight. He saw Dionysia approaching, wrinkled his brows, and
with a gesture of command indicated that she
was to go away. But she did not let this deter
her; she walked straight toward him, and before he could recover from his surprise snatched
the pipe out of his hand, broke it in two, and
hurled the pieces at his feet. Now for the first
time he seemed to come to his senses, and he
seized Dionysia by the wrists, and was about
to throw her on the ground. She defended
herself and resisted; his glowing eyes were fixed
angrily on hers, his quick breath blew over her
forehead. He compressed his lips; she laughed.
Suddenly he let go of her hands, and flung both
arms around her body. A surge of anger rose
in her and she wished to tear herself free. But
as he drew her more and more powerfully toward himself, she herself pressed closer, weak-
ened, sank down on the grass, and with unsus-
pected joy gave herself to his fierce kisses. . .

For many days she now wandered through
the open country with the shepherd and his
flock. During hot noondays they rested under

the shadow of trees; at night they slept on lonely meadows. The flock, accustomed to follow the tune of the shepherd's pipe, which now seemed to have grown silent forever, slowly scattered, and finally nothing but a single little lamb skipped along beside the pair.

After a hundred days of sunshine and a hundred starlit nights, there came an overcast morning. A harsh wind tore across the meadow on which the lovers had slept, and Dionysia awoke trembling.

"Wake up," she called out to the shepherd, "and rise. I am cold. Far away in the morning mist I see houses; the road here leads down there. Go quickly, buy me shoes, dress, and cloak."

The shepherd rose, drove the last little lamb before him, sold it in the city, and for the money received brought Dionysia what she had desired. When Dionysia was newly garbed, she stretched out on the ground again, crossed her arms above her head, and said:

"Now, I should like to hear you blow some melody on your pipe again."

"I no longer have a pipe," replied the shepherd. "You broke it."

"You should have held it more firmly,"

replied Dionysia. Then she looked around and asked: "Where is our silver-fleeced retinue?"

"It scattered when it no longer heard the tune of my pipe," replied the youth.

"Why did you not take better care?" asked Dionysia.

"I cared for nothing but you," replied the youth.

"But this morning a little lamb was still resting beside us."

"I sold it to bring you shoes, dress, and cloak."

"Would you hadn't been obedient to me," said Dionysia with vexation and rose and turned away.

"Where do you intend to go?" asked the shepherd, painfully surprised.

"Home," replied Dionysia, and she felt a faint yearning for Erasmus.

"It is a long distance," said the shepherd. "You will never find the way alone; I will accompany you."

"You don't imagine that I mean to go all that long distance on foot."

At the same moment a carriage was passing below on the highway. Dionysia called loudly, and beckoned with her hand. But the driver paid no attention, whipped up the horses, and urged them on. Dionysia called more loudly yet. Then some one leaned out of the carriage window and turned toward the direction from which the voice sounded. When he became aware of the beautiful woman, he ordered the driver to stop, stepped from the carriage, and went to meet Dionysia, who was hastening down the slope of the meadow.

"What do you wish," he asked. "Why did you call and beckon?"

"I beg of you," replied Dionysia, "to give me a place in your carriage, and to take me to my home." And she named the place where her husband's house was.

"Gladly I shall fulfill your wish, most beautiful lady," replied the stranger, "but it is a long way to your home, and as I am just returning from a journey, it is necessary that I spend a day at my home to look after my affairs. In the rooms of my house you shall find welcome, and before you set out on the journey home, a day's and a night's rest might refresh you."

Dionysia was satisfied; the traveler graciously opened the carriage door, and let the young woman enter. She leaned in a corner without once looking around, and he sat down by her side. The carriage started to move again. At first it went on along the highway between green countrysides; then it continued between rows of small, well-kept houses.

"Where are we?" asked Dionysia.

"All this that you see here," replied the stranger, "belongs to me. I build engines for all the country, and in the villages through which we are passing dwell the workingmen whom I employ." While he was saying these words, Dionysia looked at him more closely, and saw that his small lips were tense with restrained power, and that his clear eyes were proud and looked straight ahead as if inexorable.

When night broke the carriage stopped in front of a house which was like a castle. The gate opened. A marble-white hall gleamed under many lights. At her master's signal a girl appeared, and led Dionysia into a comfortably furnished apartment. She helped her undress, and then pointed to an adjoining room which was of crystalline blue. Here a bath was made ready; with delight Dionysia plunged into its tepid flood. Later the girl reappeared, and asked whether she desired to dine alone or

in company with the gentleman. Dionysia
explained that for to-day she would prefer to
stay by herself, for she already knew that she
would remain here for a time long enough to
become as intimately acquainted with her host
as she might desire.

III

It was autumn when Dionysia had entered
the castle; spring was approaching, and she
still lingered, no longer as guest, but as the
consort of the master, and as mistress of the
house. From her balcony there was an unob-
structed outlook upon a broad rolling country.
From distant trough-like valleys chimneys
rose; the wind brought with it the sound of
whirring wheels and beating hammers, and on
dark evenings, above the tall flues flying sparks
glowed and died out in the air. Crowded close
to the castle, very near one another and surrounded by scanty little gardens, dwelling
houses stood in long rows; a thick forest separated even these that were nearest from the
castle. Beyond the last factory buildings cul-
tivated fields struggled up the hillside and
sloped down again toward invisible plains.

Distant columns of smoke, however, betrayed
the fact, that a sphere of industry extended
even beyond the hills.

The castle itself stood in a park of such wide
extent that Dionysia, who had formed the
habit of walking there every day, even in the
last days of winter still found undiscovered
spots. Sometimes at the noonday hour or in
the evening the master accompanied her on her
walks, and she learned from him that scarcely
two decades ago this park had been a sort of
primeval wilderness. Where the castle now
stood there had been a little house, and down
below, where a hundred chimneys now smoked,
one poor forge, alone among the peasants' huts,
had been at work. Everything which since
then had sprung up meant no more than the
beginning of a greater work. Things were
already stirring on the edges of the hill-country;
swampy regions were being drained; streams
were endowed with resistance and new power
by channels and dams; the forests were being
thinned out. During the coming summer a
huge exhibition hall was to be ready to hold the
models of all the engines that had ever gone
from here out into the world and of all that
were to go in the future.

Guests often appeared at the castle: invent-
ors, architects, representatives of the ruling
prince, envoys of foreign states. Some went
away contented and in a happy frame of mind;
others, ill at ease and perplexed. The master's
word always seemed to have the same grave
importance and weight. Dionysia always felt
that not one of the guests had ever been able
to gain an advantage over him; always he had
been wiser and stronger than all the others.

Sometimes she herself wandered by his side
among the glowing hammers and the whirling
wheels, the shifting belts and the humming
rollers. Nor did she remain a stranger to the
offices, where drawings and plans were made,
letters received and dispatched, and the books
of the house were kept. The master seemed
to consult with every draftsman and every
workingman; everywhere he was teacher and
pupil at the same time. Out of whatever door
he stepped he always knew more definitely
what was thought or done in the room he just
left than those who spent all their days there.

On many an evening artists, both in song and
on various instruments, were heard. Even an
excellent company of actors occasionally gave
performances in the castle, at which spectators

from the immediate vicinity and also from
further away were present. Thus provision
was made to keep every one of Dionysia's hours
free from even a suspicion of emptiness; yet
her right to solitude was completely preserved.
The master never neglected to ask whether his
presence might be welcome, and when it pleased
Dionysia to walk alone, it needed only a nod to
free her from all company.

Once at the beginning of summer she was
wandering through a little village; though three
hours distant, it was still included among the
master's possessions. A pale little girl ran out
to meet her, and with outstretched hands
begged for a morsel of bread. Dionysia, surprised, shook her head, and was inclined to
regard the child as a forward, beggarly creature
of which there might be some even here. Then
a sad, timid expression in the eyes of the girl
made her thoughtful, and she decided she herself would look in at the house. A woman, no
longer young, stood in the entrance, a child in
her arms; two others were playing on the floor
with bits of wood and the seeds of fruit. To
Dionysia's question the woman replied that the
only food the little beggar had had to-day was
half a glass of milk. Without waiting for fur-

ther questions she gave free rein to her complaints, and so Dionysia learned that in this village, at least among the families blessed with children, poverty and distress were familiar guests. Dionysia was exceedingly surprised, left all the money she had with her, and hurried home to inform him whom she loved of the conditions she had found. She was convinced that the faithlessness and evil intent of subordinate officials alone were responsible.

The master enlightened her. Even under the simplest and apparently most equitable circumstances the lives of individuals were shaped most diversely according to personal characteristics and all manner of accidents. He advised her not to concern herself in the future about such matters. She declared that she was unable to follow this advice, and begged for permission to remove, or at least relieve, in her own way, and as far as lay in her power, the evil conditions under which not the guilty alone suffered. The master had no objection to her using the sums which were so abundantly at her disposal in whatever manner she deemed best, and he interposed no protest of any sort to the investigations and explorations which she began to undertake the very next day.

She soon noticed that the need for help was greater than she had ever suspected, and that, even where the present seemed to be free from care, a dark and uncertain future loomed. But it was just where the people seemed to be reasonably comfortable that the unconscious hopelessness of their existence filled Dionysia with amazement and sorrow. She finally reached the point where she felt her own over-abundance in everything as an injustice toward these to whom even the necessities were denied. She soon understood that even if here and there from one day to the next, she might make some one's lot more happy, the order of the state, yea, even the laws of the world, would have to be changed to bring about complete and permanent help. Sadly she discontinued her explorations, and neither social pleasures, which were offered in greater and more vivid abundance than ever before, nor the tenderness of her lover could overcome her melancholy.

At this time rumors told of a growing discontent among the laboring population; the master, without a word of reproach, did not conceal from Dionysia the fact that she might be in part to blame for this movement, the like of which had never before occurred in this

region, not only on account of the charity
which she had formerly practised, but also on
account of its unexpected cessation. Delega-
tions appeared at the castle to demand increase
in wages and decrease in the hours of work.
Some of the demands the master was able to
grant in proportion as his own prosperity had
increased. A period of quiet set in, but it did
not last long. New, more excessive demands
were made, and had to be denied. The unrest
increased, turned into bitterness; in some dis-
tricts there was cessation of work, and soon the
rebels forced a closing down, where up to that
time work had continued. Deeds of violence
occurred; the master was compelled to seek aid
from the government; soldiers came, bitterness
grew, and engagements followed with victims
on both sides. The power of the state soon
won complete victory. Several of the leaders
of the movement were thrown into prison,
others dismissed; new forces of labor, gathered
from everywhere, were engaged, and it did not
take long before the wheels turned, the chimneys poured forth smoke, and the machines
pounded again throughout the countryside.

During these difficult times Dionysia had
remained in seclusion. She had feared for

the master, who was always to be found where
the danger was greatest. But at the same
time she was unhappy over the lot of the
weak, whose revolt she thought she understood better than anyone else. Whatever way
the decision would fall, Dionysia foresaw that
it would not bring her peace; and on the day
of decision, when her lover returned as victor
to the castle, he found Dionysia no longer
there. Poor and free as she had come, she
set out on her journey home, firm in the
belief that there was nothing now that could
still tempt her.

IV

The uprising seemed to have been quelled
in the place on which Dionysia turned her
back, but it had moved on more decisively
to others, nearby and further away; it seized
upon ever new circles, and spread through
the entire country. Soon not only the workingmen stood in rebellion against the factory
owners, but also the poor against those that
had possessions, those that were subjects
against those that were free, the citizenry
against the nobility. So it happened that on
the third day of her journey Dionysia fell in

with a sort of military camp. It was a rabble
of men, women, half-grown youths, children,
some of them armed with the strangest of
weapons. Being well-dressed she was stopped.
She declared that she was on the way home.
It was easy for her to prove that she had with
her only money enough barely to cover her
needs. An older man, who had at once taken
her part against the unseemly jests of the
younger, made her thoughtful when he pointed
out that the roads were insecure. She really
ought to be glad that she had been stopped
here, where, in spite of all the injustice that
had been endured, the desire for revenge had
not yet degenerated into a blind rage for
destruction and slaughter. He advised her
for the time being to remain here; for the
present she would be assured of every pro-
tection; to continue her journey might expose
her, a beautiful young woman traveling alone,
to dangers worse than death.

Dionysia followed his advice the more will-
ingly because it was not difficult for her to
foresee with what hostility any resistance
would be received. She soon observed that
she was among determined but not irresponsible people. They were miners who, until

a few days before, had spent their lives in the
darkness and amid the deadly fumes of deep
pits. All the crew, habituated as they were
to perpetual night, were filled with the most
extravagant hopes; it was as if their blood
and senses had become intoxicated by the
light of heaven. All counted on the defeat of
the mighty, to whom they had hitherto been
bondservants; they counted on the understanding and bond of brotherhood of the wise
and on the establishment of a realm of justice
and equality. Dionysia, feeling as if some
higher power had put her in her present position, declared that she shared their faith,
and that she was ready to suffer with her new
companions, whatever fate might have in store
for them—victory or downfall.

The first night she slept undisturbed in the
separate camp of the women and children.
On the following day the men held council,
and soon there were rumors of division and
conflict. Some held that it would be wisest
to enter into negotiations with the authorities
who had grown hesitant; others, more im-
patient, proposed without delay to invade the
next city in the manner of an enemy. Finally
it was decided to send people out to neighbor-

ing groups of insurrectionists, first of all to
discover how matters stood here and there.
The messengers went; not a single one returned
in the evening, not one on the next morning.
Those who remained behind had a feeling of
impending evil.

At noon the entire band set into motion,
men, women, and children. On the horizon
columns of smoke and red reflections of fire
appeared. They wandered through a wide,
barren plain where water and food were
lacking. They passed through miserable,
almost wholly deserted villages, and broke
into cellars and farmyards where spoil of
wine and foodstuffs was taken, though indeed
not in sufficient quantity. Those that were
thirsty fell upon those that were drunken;
those that were hungry upon those that had
eaten their fill. All order was dissolved; men
and women encamped during the night in
utter confusion.

A haggard young man, who during the
day's journey had already attached himself
to Dionysia, approached her and drew her
away with him; in the bushes he embraced
her with greedy arms, and she belonged to
him this one night. In the morning he no

longer knew her, and as far as she was concerned he disappeared as one of the crowd to
whom she was wholly indifferent.

They wandered on, past smoking farms and
burned villages, through a dead and devastated
country. Finally the host halted before the
dark silent walls of a city with closed gates.
No one knew what the following day might
bring forth; heaven and earth were veiled
in mystery; not a torch was lighted; silence
lay heavily over the dark multitude. Suddenly
shrill laughter sounded out of the darkness
as if to pierce the horror which could no
longer be borne. A raging cry followed the
laughter, and after the cry came stifled groans,
woeful howls, and then laughter again. Men
and women had crowded close together,
inextricably; every one took the one nearest
him, not one of them resisted, for of a sudden
they knew that the morrow would end everything.

Dionysia was seized by a terrible fear. She
succeeded in groping her way further and
further away among tense grasping hands and
hot dry breaths, and finally escaped. Throughout the night she crouched, wrapped in her
torn cloak, in the shelter of a projecting wall,

where the groans and screams and laughter reached her only hoarsely and faintly. Suddenly at the first gray of dawn the gates of the city flew open. Armed men stormed out, and fell upon those that were exhausted, dissipated, drunken with sleep—fell upon men and women, cut them to pieces and drove into the city whomsoever the whim of their murderous steel had spared. Dionysia was among those; and before sunrise she lay with hundreds of other women in the court of a fortress behind a gate that had crashed shut. She was shaken by fever, seized by wild, incomprehensible dreams, and finally her senses left her.

V

She awoke in a spacious white room. A nurse sat at her head; from her she learned that she had been brought hither from the prison and had lain unconscious for many days. She heard, too, that the uprising throughout the country had been suppressed, that many of the guilty were languishing in prison, and that some had been executed. And finally the nurse told her that a young officer, a count, had assumed responsibility for her, because her appearance had convinced him that she could have fallen among the rebels and prisoners through no fault of her own and only by some strange accident. With a significant smile the nurse added that the count called daily to inquire after her; he often stayed at her bedside a long time, and watched her with deep emotion. An old physician entered the sickroom, and did not manifest any special surprise when he found Dionysia conscious. He had expected the turn on the present day, and undertook an examination of the patient. He obviously avoided every question in regard to Dionysia's origin and adventures, and established the likelihood of an early complete recovery. He then rose, took leave with elaborate courtesy, and in the hall met a young man in brilliant uniform. With a friendly but authoritative manner he seemed to refuse him entrance, and then the door closed behind the two. But there had been sufficient time for Dionysia to catch an eager glance from the light eyes of a man. As out of a dream she remembered that these same eyes had rested on her, when in a raging

fever and out of her senses she had been led
to prison between raised spears and through
echoing streets.

From day to day she felt herself grow
stronger. Gradually her thoughts too became
clear again, but she still saw no one except
the nurse and the physician. In a certain
confidential way he hinted at secret friends
who took a very warm interest in the fate of
the patient, but admission had to be firmly
denied, especially in these days of gradual
recovery. Dionysia listened to all this with
indifference. She was determined that as soon
as she was fully restored she would continue
her interrupted journey home. She intended
to stand before her husband, tell him of what
had befallen her, and ask him whether, remembering his words, and whether in spite
of all that had occurred to her, he was still
ready to receive her in his house. But at
the heart of this resolution she felt more
curiosity than desire. The idea of seeing
Erasmus again lured her as a new adventure,
not as the end of her changeful pilgrimage.

On the morning when she rose out of bed
the first time, she looked down into a little
garden from the balcony of her room. She

let her glance sweep further over the fields
that had been trampled down and choked.
The young count entered and apologized for
everything that had been done. He had taken
the responsibility with the best intentions
though without any authority. Dionysia
thanked him sincerely, but without expressing
surprise. In view of so much kindness she
declared she felt it her duty to explain who
she was. But following a sudden impulse she
gave a name that never had been hers, mentioned as her home a small city in which she
had never lived, and attributed to her husband
a profession in which he had never been
engaged. She herself was surprised at the
new pleasure she felt in lying, and it grew as
she listened to her own words. She told how
she had been a guest at the country-house of
friends. On the way back she had been
dragged from her carriage by a rebel band.
They had robbed her, and she had only been
able to save her life by confessing herself to
be a secret adherent of the insurrectionists.
For many days she had roved through the
land with these horrible creatures, and in the
end, though innocent, would have been compelled to share their fate. But now it was

time for her to return home, and so her expression of gratitude would simultaneously have to be her good-by.

The young count was downcast, but had become so accustomed to his subsidiary rôle, or was so shy naturally, that he did not attempt to oppose her. He merely begged as a last favor that he might be permitted to secure a good carriage for Dionysia's homeward journey. She had an intense wish to hear the low, quivering voice of the count speak tenderer words, but found so much pleasure in the novelty of dissimulating that she seized the count's hand as if filled with overflowing gratitude. She looked at him with her eyes, and was pleased to see that she could make them gleam with moist luminosity or grow dark and sombre just as she wished. Immediately after the count had gone, she made her preparations for leaving. The physician came and seemed displeased at her intentions. He declared he would not assume responsibility. She might very soon be compelled to interrupt her journey, and lie ill for many days and nights at whatever miserable inn there happened to be on the spot. Dionysia, quite aware that the physician was acting in collusion with the count, at first made a strong feint at opposition, then at hesitation, and finally promised with a sigh that she would accommodate herself to his arrangements whose reasonableness was quite apparent to her.

In the evening the young count returned. Since her departure had been postponed, he proposed that Dionysia should occupy a modest hunting-lodge which he owned, and stay amid the fresh breezes of the forest until her recovery was complete. She would have as companion a lady of best reputation, to avoid from the very beginning any possibility of evil report. Dionysia replied that she felt security and strength enough in and by herself, but declared that she would accept the count's invitation only on the condition that he would agree not to visit the hunting-lodge while she stayed there. The count bowed his head low as if in sign of complete submission, but she could barely restrain herself from holding out her arms and drawing him close to her breast.

On the following morning she took possession of the hunting-lodge. It was simply and neatly fitted out, and lay in solitude under

shadowy leaves, two hours away from the
city. A pretty peasant-girl was there to
receive Dionysia and to look after her further
needs; she was silent and attentive. The
food was of excellent flavor and well prepared;
the bed was delicious and soft. On the well-
kept paths beneath the tall cool tree-tops,
Dionysia wandered undisturbed as if in an
inclosed park. She often lay for hours on an
open meadow with arms crossed beneath her
head and half-closed eyes lost in the dizzy
blue of the heavens. Butterflies, flitting by,
touched her forehead, the cool breath of the
forest passed over her eyelids and hair, and
every sound of the world faded away in distant
dales.

One morning, when Dionysia was about to
leave the house, heavy clouds gathered and
hung in dark silence over the trees. Dionysia
went back and forth in the low rooms, walked
up and down in front of the door, and an ach-
ing depression rose in her soul. At noon she
did not touch any of the food. The girl found
her in tears at the set table, and received no
answer to her questions. She was frightened
and sent to the city for the count who had
confided the beautiful lady to her care. Late

in the evening, when the long sultriness at last broke in a storm with hail, thunder, and lightning, the young count, who had been so eagerly looked for, entered the room unexpectedly. He was overjoyed when Dionysia, with shining eyes and joyous welcome, flung herself upon his breast, for he had feared to find her troubled in spirit or fallen ill again.

But in the twilight of this very night on which she had given herself to him, Dionysia told him that this their first night would also have to be their last. With the quickly aroused jealous curiosity of one who had possessed, the count urged her to explain. Dionysia, driven by an uncontrollable impulse to torment her lover, asserted that suddenly she had a vague memory of having been taken by not one but many of her wild companions in that terrible night before the gates of the walled city. It seemed as if the deadening fever had already fallen on her, and she had given herself unresistingly, though with a feeling of horror. But at the same time she held out the possibility, that all this might have been only a horrible dream which in her memory now lay upon her like an unbearable truth. The young count fell into despair,

from deepest despair into new passion, from
the height of passion into raging fury; he
swore he would kill her on the spot. Finally
he pleaded merely for the one thing that she
would not leave him, for without her he
deemed his existence from this hour on would
be useless and wretched.

Dionysia stayed, and soon her soul belonged
completely to the count. She grew ashamed
of all her lies, began to suffer under them, and
finally felt the wish rising within her to tell
her lover the true history of her life. But
afraid of rousing new distrust by her belated
confession, she postponed it from day to day.

On an autumn day, heavy with rain, a
messenger on horseback appeared, bearing the
news, that on the frontier the long-expected
movements of the neighboring army were
becoming more and more threatening. He
showed orders commanding the count to take
his place at the head of his regiment within
the next twenty-four hours. As soon as the
messenger had ridden off at full speed, Dionysia
declared to her lover that under no circumstances would she leave his side; it was her
irrevocable intention to go to war with him,
dressed as a man. This touched the young

count deeply and made him very happy, but at first he tried to show Dionysia the impossibility of such an attempt. When, however, she swore that if worst came to worst she nevertheless would follow him and his fate, even against his will—yes, even join the camp-followers of the army—he left the hunting-lodge with her for the city on the very same day.

He begged for an audience with the prince, who had always been well-disposed toward him. With all due deference he put the case before him for decision. The prince, himself wedded to a young and noble spouse, was by nature as easily moved to wrath as to enthusiasm. Any sort of strange whim always quickly captivated him. As the times were so unsettled, he found no objection to the execution of a plan which though daring was also heroic. Thus it befell that on the following morning Dionysia rode through the city's gate by her lover's side. She was in a soldier's garb, but not disguised, rather regarded with high respect and sympathy. She passed through the disturbed country to the frontier, and sooner than she anticipated dashed into the midst of a skirmish. Her senses scarcely comprehended it; like a tattered red cloud it drifted about her white brow and her gleaming sword.

The war went its bloody and changeful way. By her lover's side Dionysia penetrated further into the hostile territory. She rested on earth that had been laid waste and harried by fire, was called to battle by bugles, saw men wounded and fall by her side, and wounded in the temple lay herself for many days and nights in a tottering temporary shelter among moaning and dying men. She recovered; found her lover again, after having been without any news of him, on the evening before a decisive day. Like her, his wounds were scarcely healed, but at the head of his decimated troops he was ready for new deeds of valor. At the gray of dawn they rode together into the hostile throng. They had equal share of danger and honor, and they bore home to the victorious camp a flag which they had captured together.

In the night which followed this day and which was dark and sultry, under the twofold obscurity of a starless sky and of a tent with heavy folds, Dionysia slept for the first time since the beginning of the war by the side of the young count as his wife. In the morning both stepped into the open as companions in arms, and were greeted by their comrades with voices confident with victory.

Calm sunlight lay on the plain, and out on the field among the waving helmet crests and the gleaming points of the swords, there was a feeling that the illustrious prince was nigh. But suddenly, instead of the expected message of peace, the familiar signals of approaching attack were heard. Behind a low hill clouds of dust rose, came nearer, trumpets and pipes sang out, and, mounted on black horses, a horde of wild horsemen rushed forward. Those who were so unexpectedly attacked swiftly put themselves in readiness for violent defence, and it soon appeared that it was only a small troop of foolhardy young men who opposed them. They were men determined to risk their lives on a last throw for the sake of a great stake rather than accept a dishonorable peace. But since their companions in the rear hesitated, they were quickly surrounded and cut down to the last man. But they did not sell their lives cheaply; among those who had been overthrown by their desperate attack was the young count.

Dionysia supported his wounded head on her knees. As his last drops of blood flowed over her motionless fingers, white flags fluttered round about on the heights and trumpet-blasts announced the cessation of hostilities. And as her lover's eyes broke, the exultant news of the hardly-won peace fell upon Dionysia's ears.

Where she was, however, even the loudest and deepest rejoicing grew subdued. The circle of those who rejoiced and were happy drifted further and further away from her. The prince himself, who rode hither at noon-time, greeted her from a respectful distance. She sat motionless in the full apparel of war, but without her helmet and with loosened hair which flowed over the face of her dead lover like a blue-black shroud. It was only with the coming of evening that she rose, clasped the dear corpse around the body, and with superhuman strength tied it fast in full armor to the saddle of his steed. Then she mounted hers and gave it the spurs. The other, with its dead master in the saddle, according to old habit stayed by her side. Thus the strange pair rode in silence, at a distance, from the military hosts that were

drawing homeward. The pair rode past the
hosts at full speed through the conquered
territory of the enemy towards home, and they
watched it with amazed dread.

When Dionysia had caught sight of the
towers of the city, she took the familiar by-
way to the little hunting-lodge. Its door was
open and no one was there, but it seemed to
be waiting for her. She leaped from the horse,
unbound her dead companion from the saddle,
and made ready the grave. She laid her
lover in it with sword, armor, and helmet,
and then threw earth over the body. Not
until she had accomplished this task did she
take off her own armor, and she sank into a
long deep sleep of three days and three nights.
When she awoke the young count's mother
stood at her head, tearless, and kissed the
hands that had dug her son's grave.

VI

Autumn passed on like a storm-wind,
winter slipped by. Dionysia knew that since
the night preceding the last battle a new
being was growing within her. So she felt
herself bound with a new hope both to her
departed lover and to life.

In spring she gave birth to a boy, and when he drank for the first time at her breast, the first smile flitted over Dionysia's face. Precious gifts from the count's mother, from other relatives, from the prince himself, were laid in the cradle of the hero's son. When Dionysia left her bed, she felt for the first time as if she had to dress in white again; in light, mobile folds, like those of her fragrant gown, she felt the flood of the mellow, flower-laden day about her. Above her young head, where already dwelt so many things she remembered and so many she had forgotten, hung a blue spring, fresh like life itself, pregnant with the future. She did not yet throw herself into the stream of life, but she let its flood come up to her very feet.

A festival celebrated by the folk of the land took place not far away. She watched with lively interest a round dance held on the forest meadow. At first a certain awe kept them at a distance from the widow of the hero, who was herself a heroine. But soon she accepted the homage laid at her feet by the enthusiastic youth of the land. Even the unexplained mystery of her origin lay like a golden gleam over her lauded brow.

Toward the beginning of winter she moved into the count's castle, which was regarded as naturally belonging to her. She lived there in quiet retirement, at first devoting herself entirely to maternal duties. Finally, however, the doors opened; in the beginning only to the count's relatives, but later also to the family connections and more distant friends. Soon there was no one in the country, either of high birth or merit, who would have failed in expressing his admiration and love for her mysterious and high nobility. That the prince himself also appeared surprised no one. Touched by Dionysia's enigmatic charm he came again. The glamour of his power passed from his youthful eyes into her newly awakened senses. Like a dream, the proud consciousness of her extraordinary lot overflowed from her into his blood, and none of the scruples to which lesser personalities are subject restrained the wishes of either, and the prince, forgetting his wedded wife, offered Dionysia the glowing gift of his love.

At first this turn of affairs was accepted in the neighborhood and throughout the country without hostility or derogatory report. Many, indeed, not alone flatterers and courtiers, acquiesced in it as something natural and permissible. The first to turn away, surprised, but silent, was the count's mother. Several relatives followed her example, and from that time avoided Dionysia's presence. Not till then did the more intimate circle of the princess begin to show disapproval, while the princess herself still regarded the prince's relations to the strange woman as only friendly.

But when the truth became known to her, she, hurt in her innermost being, shut herself away from her husband without the utterance of a word. He, as if on purpose, from now on proudly and openly began to show his love for Dionysia before all the people. He no longer suffered her to dwell in the castle she had inherited from the count, but made ready as habitation for her one of the princely estates close to the city.

From now on he not only devoted his hours of leisure to his mistress, but also received ministers and ambassadors in her apartments. Councils concerning the state and the people were held in her presence, and soon her voice had a share in every decision. All who were close to the throne bowed before her and without reserve accepted whatever influence the

prince delegated to her. For this reason she
might have regarded herself as the true ruling
princess of the country had she not sometimes
noticed, when out driving and oftener from
day to day, that people she met seemed not
to notice her or even intentionally turned
away. At first she took this lightly and
smiled, regarding it the envy and folly of
mean souls, but gradually anger raised its
head in her and increased. One day, when
she rode past a young nobleman famous as
a supporter of the deserted princess, she saw
him look up at her, the prince's mistress,
with a contemptuous curl of the lips, and
she struck him in the face with her whip.
When in his rage he hurled a vile word of
abuse into her face, she had him put under
arrest. It was her intercession alone that
made the indignant prince revoke the death
penalty from the giver of this heedless insult.

But after this episode the bitterness of the
two factions, which hitherto had lurked in
silence, turned into open and violent hostility.
Reports were carried to Dionysia as to what
was being said about her among the people,
among the nobility, and particularly among
those that formed the immediate entourage

of the princess. She, who only a short time ago had seemed a stranger, enigmatic but perhaps sent by Divine Providence, to-day was regarded by many as nothing better than an adventuress and a harlot. No serious danger, however, yet threatened her; the prince stood by her more firmly than ever. In defiance of the growing opposition, of his own free will he enlarged Dionysia's powers in every direction, surrounded her with a hitherto unheard-of magnificence, and invested her five-year-old son with the title of prince, and pinned on the child's breast an order which previously had been granted only to members of the royal house.

Every careless word, every dubious gesture, which seemed to be directed at Dionysia, was punished with terrible rigor. Dionysia herself was no longer inclined to ask mercy of the prince for people of high or low degree who had transgressed against the belief in her majesty. When she drove through the streets in her golden carriage, drawn by six black horses, accompanied by outriders before and behind, she heard the false and forced notes in the cheers that greeted her. She felt that they no longer meant respect, but that sober dread and fear and hatred were weaving a web about her. Evil dreams of conspiracies and plots disturbed her sleep, even at the side of the prince, though it seemed he wished to protect her with his own body.

A rumor began to run through the palace, that evil designs against Dionysia were being hatched among the entourage of the cast-off princess. No one knew whence it came, but Dionysia deemed the time was ripe to demand peremptory redress from her lover. When he hesitated, she put before him the choice, either to banish his wedded wife from the court and to exile her from the country, or to let her herself go whenever and whithersoever she wished.

Since no definite proofs of a conspiracy existed, servile courtiers felt they were justified in manufacturing them artificially. A trial having every appearance of regularity was held; the suspected princess was found guilty in her absence, and was ordered to depart from court and country and to leave behind all her papers and jewels. On the following morning, as if she had long been prepared for this, she set out accompanied by a few of the faithful on the journey to the

distant realm of her royal parents. Others,
however, who were suspected were expelled
from the country; and some, indeed, who
were regarded as specially dangerous, disappeared in the seemingly insatiable prisons
of the country. Since even the slightest sign
of dissatisfaction was punished relentlessly,
tranquillity came upon the country, and
Dionysia finally became a sovereign with a
power so absolute that it could hardly have
been greater had she borne the crown upon
her head.

But the higher her power rose, the less joy
she took in her lot. The festivals held in her
honor grew noisier and noisier, but lacked
every element of spontaneity. Even raptur-
ous hours in the prince's arms grew shallow
and turbid. Soon Dionysia recognized that
her deepest wish had been for her lover to
have resisted her vain desires, and she began
to despise him because he had obeyed her
every wish. To humiliate him in the way it
seemed to her he deserved, she gave herself
on the royal couch to such of the young men
of the court who at the moment pleased her.
In shame and penitence the prince at first
kept his wrath locked within his heart, but

soon his senses grew feverish and confused
and he surrendered himself to the easily won
favors of other women. The gates of the
palace began to open for them as once they
had for Dionysia. But, as if in revenge for
this, those young men rose most quickly to
highest honor at court who knew best how to
flatter Dionysia's greedy desires. Unbridled,
heedless of everything, shamelessly, life went
on in the palace. Soon it was rumored among
the people that the gigantic torches in the
festal halls went out on many a night as if
ashamed of the excess of outrageous lusts
with which the prince and his mistress, the
paramours and the courtesans regaled themselves.

On a gray morning, with a shimmering
cloak thrown lightly about her naked shoulders,
with face veiled to escape the pursuit of a
company of drunken men, Dionysia fled from
the hall, where the prince himself, like one
suddenly become mad, raved aimlessly hither
and thither with a drawn knife. She ran
down the stairs, in obedience to a call which
she thought was her last, and hurried toward
a murky pool beneath the beech-trees at the
end of the park. There she wanted to drown

her debauch, her dishonor, her disgust with her
past life, all three together, and for all eternity.

But when she saw her distorted image in the
shimmering water, she remembered what for
two years she had scarcely given a thought to:
namely, that she was a mother. She turned,
and under the drooping limbs hurried back
toward the palace. As if carried by the wings
of youth, she strode into the bedchamber of the
seven-year-old prince. Without any other
thought than to take him in her arms and with
her into death, she had stepped up to his bedside. But when she saw him slumbering so
quietly, his sweet childish brow seemed luminous with a wondrous majesty which she had
never before noticed. Immediately another
impulse flashed into her mind, and in coming
into being became so potent that she took the
sleeping prince in her arms. Barefooted, she
hurried back to the hall of the feast. Here she
found the prince, alone, unarmed, with tangled
hair hanging over his forehead; he sat with
terrible solemnity at the disordered table, covered with half-withered flowers.

She knew at this moment that he was filled
with the same hunger for death as she herself.
When he saw Dionysia standing before him

with the sleepy-eyed prince, he looked at her
for a long time and asked the reason of this
strange appearance. She held out the child
toward him like a precious gift, and demanded
that on this very day he recognize him as heir
to the throne. And when he was silent with
surprise, she swore under the vivifying gleam
of the new sun which was just rising, that the
horrible lustful latter-day life would now come
to an end. She was determined hereafter to
devote herself wholly to works of well-doing
and law-giving, and to dwell by his beloved
side as a faithful consort.

She was confident of being strong enough to
wipe out the dishonor of the past years in the
glory of those that were to come. She was sure
that in the memory of the people the recollec-
tion of the years that had gone by would per-
sist only vaguely, like the memory of a great
illness, and finally become no more than a
legend. Having her son declared heir was to
be the last act of absolutism, and it seemed
justified to her since in every way it was to
redound to the country's advantage. The
prince with a new light in his eyes agreed.

Without delay the council of nobles was
called together. With passionate gravity the

prince expressed his wish, and no opposition was voiced. The news was proclaimed among the people, and the preparations had been carefully made so that it would be received with rejoicing. In the evening lights flamed in all windows, crowds which seemed filled with joyous excitement swept through the streets, and in so far as one could overhear what was being said, it seemed just as if on this day a noble wife had borne to a beloved ruler a long-desired heir.

For the first time in a long while Dionysia allowed herself to be deceived. Though the expressions of rejoicing on the part of the turbulent crowd were either bought or the result of fear, she looked at them as a newly awakened hope in the heart of a warm-hearted populace whose favor had never been wholly lost and so could speedily be regained.

Her heart filled with joy, she stepped out on the balcony before which stood a densely massed multitude. The populace called more and more insistently for sight of the prince, as if it were their right to see the heir of the realm face to face this great day on which his high destiny had been decided. Filled with new happiness, Dionysia hurried to the chambers

of her son. She hardly noticed that the guard
which usually stood at the door was absent.
She hurried on. Then she saw the governess
of the prince lying in the entrance like one who
was drunken. Seized by evil foreboding,
Dionysia rushed to her son's bed and found
him with broken eyes and distorted face, a deep
wound on the forehead, dead on the wet red
linen.

For a moment only Dionysia stood be-
numbed, then she seized the body of her child,
plunged with it from room to room, through
halls, over stairways, through all the palace
which seemed deserted as a grave. Finally,
always with the bloody corpse of the child in
her arms, she found herself on the balcony
again, where the prince stood alone. She
showed the murdered child first to him and
then to the crowd below. With eloquent words
she appealed to them for frightful vengeance.
The prince, however, immediately hurried
away, as if he had seen a spectre. Dionysia
stood alone—and down in front of the palace,
suddenly every sound became extinguished.
No moan of anguish answered the mother's
wail, no cry of rage surged up. No one doubted
but that a judgment of God, not one that had

its source in ill-disposed people, had fallen upon
them. Any resistance would be vain, even
impious. Silent, crouching, like witnesses of a
long-expected judgment, all the thousands
slunk away and disappeared into the darkness
of the night. Dionysia's renewed screams of
horror shrilled into a void, and finally, with the
bloody corpse of the child in her arms, she sank
down on the stone flags.

When she awoke, a great silence was about
her. She was alone, and the child's body had
disappeared. For a moment she wanted to
imagine that she had awakened from a horrible
dream. The sight of her bloody hands brought
her back to reality. She rose, and looked
around and down over the balustrade. The
gray dawn crept dully over the deserted space
in front of the palace. Dionysia hurried from
room to room. Not a living creature was
visible, not a guard in the halls, not a lackey;
in the stables not a horse and not a carriage;
Dionysia was absolutely alone. The palace
seemed like a place that had been cursed, deserted by all that drew breath. An incom-
parable fear seized Dionysia, and she dared not
step out into the open. Suddenly she remem-

bered a subterranean passage which led from her sleeping room to the prince's residence.

Through a door known only to her, Dionysia stepped out into the darkness, and rushed straight ahead with her dress grazing along the walls. Gradually a faint light began to play about her; the way seemed endless. She ran as if hunted, until finally she came to another door. She thrust it open, and suddenly stood, as if cast forth out of the wall, before the prince, who, in a dark costume, sat alone at his writing table on which a candle burned. He started, his eyes flickered, he tried to conceal a sheet of paper that lay before him. She snatched at it, he let his trembling hands fall—and Dionysia read her own death-warrant, which lacked only the prince's signature.

More pitiable than she had ever seen him, divested of all dignity, he whom she had once loved stood before her, and stammered cowardly but fateful words. He had succumbed to irresistible forces, he was a prisoner within his own palace. The cast-off princess with her supporters was already on the way hither, and only if he would subscribe his name to the paper could he save himself, his country, his dominion, and perhaps his life. He was painfully surprised to see Dionysia standing before him. In his heart he had hoped she had already taken flight and found safety. Hadn't the palace been absolutely deserted? Hadn't she found the roads open in every direction? That she had not made better use of the confusion of the night was her own, incomprehensible fault. It seemed almost that intentionally she had given herself over to certain destruction.

But now she was to discover—and his speech sounded more positive and insolent with each word—that he was a merciful sovereign. He would not, as with all due reason she might fear, call the guard. No, he would rather leave her at liberty immediately to disappear through the door by which she had just entered. During the day she was to remain in the subterranean passage, and when night broke she was to escape at the other end. He would not deliver her up; indeed, he would see to it that her palace remained isolated all day. At the expiration of this period she was to take flight as quickly and as far as her feet could carry her. Finally he gave her his word as sovereign that until then she would be secure from all pursuit.

Dionysia let him talk and all the while looked

him steadily in the eyes, which always evaded
her cold glance. Then, without a word of
reply, she walked past him, who suddenly grew
pale, and pushed open the door to the reception-
room. She walked between the guards that
stood motionless, down over the marble stairway, through the high palace-gate, then
through the streets of the city, past people that
recognized her and avoided her like one that
had been branded—she walked in her blood-
soaked dress, with her half-closed eyes fixed
straight before her. A few followed her as far
as the city gate, then more and more people
gathered at a distance. Dionysia turned; with
a commanding gesture of her blood-stained
hands she forbade them to follow her further.
And now in the mellow spring air, between the
yellow fields that undulated in the morning
light, she took a deep breath and set out on the
journey home.

VII

She walked at night time, and during the day
slept in meadows and forests; she washed her
body and gown in rivers and pools, and sub-
sisted on the fruits which chance offered her.
Neither to conceal herself, nor to prolong a

life which had become a matter of indifference to her, did she follow the paths that lay apart from the main-traveled roads, but solely that she need no longer listen to the voices of men, nor see the faces of men. After a series of days of which she had kept no count, she stood on a silent, starlit midnight hour at the door of the house she had left so long ago. It was open as if awaiting her.

Without entering the house itself, Dionysia went up the winding stairs to the tower where she was sure she would find her husband. She saw him, standing erect, with his eye at the telescope which was turned toward heaven. When he heard steps he turned around, and when he recognized Dionysia his face showed no sign of surprise; there was only a mild smile of the kind which welcomes friendly guests.

"It is I," said Dionysia.

Her husband nodded. "I have been expecting you. It was on this night, neither earlier nor later, that you had to come."

"Then you know what my life has been?"

"Even though you lived it under another name, I know it. It was not of the kind that could be kept hidden. And of all living women, it was to you alone that such a fate could have been allotted. Welcome, Dionysia."

"Welcome, you say? And you feel no abhorence of me?"

"You have lived your life, Dionysia. You stand before me purer than all the others that draw breath amid the murky fumes of their desires. You know who you are. Why should I feel abhorrence of you?"

"I know who I am? I know it as little as when you let me go. Within the bounds which you at first set for me and where duty meant everything, I was unable to find myself. Into the world without bounds whither you sent me and where everything was allurement, I had to lose myself. I know not who I am."

"What do you mean, Dionysia? Are you ungrateful, and do you wish to reproach me for having done what no sage among lovers ever dared and no lover among the sages was ever strong enough to do?"

"You, a sage? And you knew not that only a narrow path is granted to every human being where he can understand and fulfill his being? There where the unique, inborn, never returning riddle of his being runs in harmony along the same channel with the highest laws of divine and human order? A lover, you? And you did not descend into the valley on that distant morning to break the pipe whose notes were threatening temptation to your beloved? Your heart was tired, Erasmus, that is why you let me go without taking up the struggle which then was not yet lost. And your spirit was strangled in the cold, claw-like clutch of words. That is why you thought it possible to capture the infinite fullness of life, the play of millions of forces in the hollow mirror of a formula."

And she turned to leave.

"Dionysia," the husband called after her. "Be yourself! Your changeful fate has brought confusion to your mind. Here you will find peace and clarity again. Have you forgotten? Chamber, bed, and gown are waiting for you, and neither question nor reproach shall ever torment you. Here you will find safety; without lurk danger and death."

Already at the door, Dionysia turned once more. "What care I for what is waiting without? I am no longer afraid of what is without. Your nearness alone makes me afraid!"

"My nearness, Dionysia? Do you imagine, I might ever forget my pledged word? Be without care, Dionysia! Here is peace, for here is understanding!"

"And in speaking thus you yourself tell me why I flee from you—? Had you felt a shudder at the breath of the thousand events that hover about my brow, I might have dared to stay. Our souls might have fused in the glow of nameless sorrows. But now, more than all the masks and miracles of the world, I dread the stony grimace of your wisdom."

At this she descended the winding stairway again, without looking back a single time. Hurriedly she left the house, and soon disappeared in the distant shadow of the plain.

After a brief numbness, Erasmus hastened after her and followed her trail for hours. But he did not overtake her, and finally had to make up his mind to return. All further search for Dionysia was vain. She had disappeared permanently. No one knows whether she lived on for a longer period somewhere in the world, perhaps under an assumed name, or whether, unrecognized, she soon came to an accidental or self-chosen end.

But not long after, Erasmus discovered a new star which gleamed mysteriously and roamed through space according to still unknown laws.

And among his papers a memorandum was
found that he had intended to call this star
Dionysia, in memory of his wife, for he bore no
lasting ill-will toward her, in spite of the cruelty
of her last words.   Other investigators searched
all the distances of heaven, at every season of
the year and at every hour; but not one of
them ever succeeded in finding the star again.
Infinity seemed to have swallowed it forever.

THE MURDERER

THE MURDERER

A YOUNG man, a doctor of both laws, without practising his profession, without parents, living in comfortable circumstances, well liked as a charming companion, had been for over a year on terms of intimacy with a young girl of humble origin. Like himself, she was without relatives, and so was in no need to consider the world's opinion in any way. Soon after the relation began, less out of kindness of heart or passion than because he felt a need for an undisturbed enjoyment of his new happiness, Alfred had induced her to give up her position as correspondent in a large Viennese business house.

For a considerable period of time, surrounded by the flattery of her tender gratitude, he had felt happier in the easy-going enjoyment of their common freedom than in any other previous relation. Now the fateful restlessness which he knew so well was beginning to grow on him. It had always indicated the approaching end of an affair of the heart, but in the present instance the end seemed still out of sight.

In his mind's eye he saw himself sharing the fate of one of the friends of his youth, who years ago had become entangled in a similar relationship, and now was forced to live the narrow and restricted life of a man of family. There were many hours which should have been filled with unalloyed joy in the presence of a soft and tender creature like Elise had it not been for presentiments like these, but now they began to bore and annoy him. He had the capacity, and, what he set greater store by, the thoughtfulness, not to let Elise become aware of such moods, but they had the effect of causing him to seek out more frequently those excellent circles from whose society he had become almost wholly estranged during the course of the past year.

When on the occasion of a dance a popular young lady, the daughter of a well-to-do manufacturer, met his advances with marked friendliness, he suddenly saw how easily a union suitable to his station and means might be arranged. The other relation, which had begun like a gay, irresponsible adventure,

began to assume the form of an irksome shackle,
and he felt that a young man of his parts was
entitled to throw it off without a second
thought.

Elise always received him with the same
serene smile; there was no change in her devo-
tion during the hours when they were together,
though these grew to be less and less frequent;
her confidence was absolute when she let him
go from her arms into a world of which she
knew nothing.

This always crowded the word of final part-
ing from his lips, even though each time before
he went he felt sure of speaking; and it filled
him with a sort of tormenting pity. The
scarcely conscious expression of this could not
but seem a new and more intimate sign of his
love to a woman of Elise's deep-seated trust-
fulness.

Thus it came to pass that Elise never believed herself more profoundly loved than when
he returned to her quiet home, that was wholly
devoted to him and his faithless love, after each
new meeting with Adele, when he was still
a-quiver with the memory of questioning looks,
hand-clasps full of promise, and the intoxication of the first secret kisses. Instead of the

good-by which even on the threshold he was determined to say, Alfred left his beloved every morning with new vows of eternal faithfulness.

Thus the days went on between the two adventures. Finally the decision was reduced to whether it would be better to choose the evening before or after his engagement to Adele for the unavoidable explanation with Elise. On the first of the two evenings, since there was still a respite, Alfred appeared at her rooms in an almost calm state of mind, so used had he become to playing double.

He found her pale, in a way he had never seen her before, leaning in a corner of the divan. On his entrance she did not rise, as was her custom, to offer him forehead and mouth as welcome. She betrayed a tired, somewhat forced smile, so that simultaneously with a feeling of relief there rose in Alfred the surmise that in some mysterious way rumors of his engagement had come to her in spite of every effort at secrecy. But in reply to his precipitate questions, he discovered only that from time to time Elise suffered from heart attacks which she had hitherto concealed from him. Usually she recovered quickly from them, but this time their after-effect threatened to last longer.

Alfred, conscious of his guilty intentions, was so deeply moved by the disclosure, that he quite outdid himself in the way of expressing his sympathy and showing his concern. Before midnight, without knowing how it had happened, he was laying out a plan for a journey for himself and Elise. It would surely bring her permanent relief from her attacks.

He had never been loved with greater tenderness and never had he been so permeated with his own tenderness, as when he left this night. On the way home he seriously considered a letter of renunciation to Adele. In explanation of his flight from his engagement and the bonds of matrimony, he meant to say that his character was unstable and did not fit him for permanent quiet and happiness. The ingenious convolutions of his sentences followed him even into his sleep. But the light of morning, playing on his bed-cover through the slits in the blinds, made the efforts he had expended seem as foolish as they were superfluous.

Indeed, it scarcely surprised him that the suffering woman of the night that had just passed

already seemed like a dream in the far distance,
like one abandoned long ago. Adele, on the
other hand, stood at the portals of his soul
a-bloom in the fragrance of immeasurable
yearning. Around the noon hour he asked
Adele's father for her hand; his offer was received courteously, but without entire assent.

Alluding with kindly irony to the many
temptations which had tried the suitor during
his youth, her father made it a condition that
Alfred should first travel a year, to test by
absence the strength and resistance of his
feelings. He opposed even the exchange of
letters between the young people, so that in this
way every possibility of self-deception might
be definitely excluded. Should Alfred return
in his present state of mind and should he find
that Adele's feelings, of which she was so sure
to-day, had not changed, he, on his side, would
not put the slightest obstacle in the way of
their immediate marriage.

Alfred received these conditions with an
appearance of reluctance, but, breathing more
easily, he really felt that fate was giving him a
new respite. After a short deliberation, he
declared that under these conditions he would
leave this very day; by so doing the term of

separation would end the sooner. Adele at
first seemed hurt by this unexpected acquies-
cence, but after a short talk alone with her,
which her father permitted, Alfred succeeded
in getting her to admire him the more because
of his wisdom in matters of love. With vows
of constancy, even with tears in her eyes, she
let him go into the dangerous distance of separation.

Alfred had scarcely reached the street before
he began to weigh every possibility that might
lead to a solution of his relations with Elise
during the course of the year which was at his
disposal. His tendency to let even the most
difficult matters of life settle themselves without active interference was very powerful, and
it not only prevailed over his vanity, but also
was favorable to the growth of gloomy fore-
bodings which his plaintive nature usually
preferred to avoid.

Under the unaccustomed necessity of living
in close intimacy all the time as was inevitable
in traveling, he thought it might happen that
Elise's love would grow cold and that she would
gradually turn from him. Her affection of the
heart also opened another possibility of liberty,
though, indeed, one he did not especially like

to think of.   Soon, however, he banished both his hopes and fears with an emphatic gesture. Finally he felt nothing but a gay, childlike anticipation of a happy journey out into the world with a tenderly devoted woman.   On the evening of the same day he babbled in the gayest of moods with the unsuspecting Elise about the alluring prospects of the impending journey.

As spring was approaching, Alfred and Elise first sought out the mellow shores of Lake Geneva. Later they went higher into the cooler mountains; the late summer they spent at an English seashore resort.   In the autumn they visited various Dutch and German cities, and finally fled the approach of cold and gloomy days, seeking the consolation of a southern sun.

Elise had never been beyond the immediate vicinity of Vienna, and so far she had flitted through this year of marvels, guided by her lover's hand, like one in a wondrous dream. However aware Alfred always was of the future and the difficulties which had been merely postponed, nevertheless the contagion of Elise's happiness seemed to have caught him and he gave himself unreservedly to the moment's delight.

At the beginning of their journey he had carefully sought to avoid meeting acquaintances; he showed himself as seldom as possible with Elise on crowded promenades or in the dining-rooms of much-frequented hotels. Later he challenged fate with a certain deliberate intention. He was almost expecting a telegram from Adele accusing him of a breach of faith. While this would have deprived him of something he still ardently desired, it would also have freed him from all internal division, all disquietude, and all responsibility. But no message nor any other news from home reached him, for Adele, contrary to Alfred's vain expectation, adhered as strictly as he himself to the conditions her father had set.

Yet the hour came, for Alfred at any rate, when this year of marvels came to a sudden end. All at once time seemed to stand still; there was no magic, everything was more desolate than anything he had ever experienced.

This happened on a bright autumn day in the Botanical Gardens at Palermo. Up to that time Elise had been in the best of health, gay and active, but suddenly both her hands went to her heart. She looked at him with fear in her eyes and immediately smiled again as if she felt it her duty not to cause her lover any trouble. Instead of touching him, this filled him with bitterness, though at first he was able to conceal it under the guise of solicitude. Without actually believing in it himself, he reproached her with having no doubt concealed several similar attacks from him. He said he was hurt, because she apparently thought him heartless. He implored her to go with him to a physician to-day, immediately, and was rather relieved when she declined the suggestion on account of her lack of confidence in the local doctors.

But when suddenly, overflowing with gratitude and love, she pressed his hand to her lips, right here, under the open sky, on the bench, while people were passing by, he felt hatred flying through his pulses like a surging wave. He was amazed at its existence, but he explained it to himself by remembering the many hours of boredom and emptiness. Of a sudden he seemed to know that their journey together had been all too full of them. At the same time a fervent wish for Adele rose like a flame in his soul. In spite of all agreements, he sent her a telegram this very day, pleading that she

send him a word to Genoa. He subscribed it:
"Eternally yours."

A few days later he found her reply in Genoa.
It read: "And I am yours for just as long."
He carried the crumpled sheet over his heart,
and, in spite of its doubtful, half-jesting tone,
it meant to him the sum and substance of all
his hopes. Then, accompanied by Elise, he
set out for Ceylon. This portion of the journey
had been left to the end, because it would
probably be the most interesting. It would
have taken a far subtler person than Elise to
have recognized that the gifts of love, richer
than ever before, which Alfred gave her, were
due solely to the vivid play of his imagination.
She did not know it was no longer she whom he
held in his arms on these dark, silent ocean
nights, but the other one, far distant, whom his
desire conjured up in all the fervency of life.

But when they finally had reached the vivid
island, he recognized in the dull uniformity of
their days that his imagination, on which too
great demands had been made, refused to serve
him any longer. He then began to avoid Elise,
and was clever enough to explain his reserve by
the renewed symptoms of heart-disease which

she showed when they first set foot on land. She accepted it, as everything that came from him, as a sign of love, which for her now contained all of life's meaning and happiness.

And when clinging closely to him and feeling entirely secure she drove under the intense glamour of a blue-golden sky through the murmuring shadows of the forest, she did not know that her companion's most intense wish was for the hour of solitude when, undisturbed by her, he might dash imploring, passionate words upon paper with his flying pen, meant for another of whose existence Elise was at that very moment unaware and always was to remain unaware. In such hours of solitude his desire for her who was absent became so powerful that he was able to forget the very lines of the face and the very voice itself of the one who was with him, belonged to him, and had traveled over the world with him for nearly a year. On the night before they set out on the journey home, coming out of the writing room, he found Elise stretched out on the bed, half-unconscious under a severe new attack. He then recognized something which hitherto he had known only as a vague fear; now he knew it like a tender, almost caressing horror. It was

the hope which had always darkly glimmered
and never wholly died in his soul.

Yet, without delay and sincerely disturbed,
he sent for the physician who appeared immediately and secured relief to the patient by a
morphine injection. The wisdom of under-
taking the journey at the present time was
doubtful, but the supposed husband declared
that for important reasons it was impossible to
postpone it. So the doctor gave him a note
recommending the patient to the special care
of the ship's doctor.

The first days out the sea-air seemed to have
an immediate salutary influence upon Elise.
Her pallor disappeared, her whole being un-
folded, her manner had less restraint than
Alfred had ever known it to have. Formerly
she had been indifferent, even hostile to any
approach on the part of strangers, no matter
how harmless it was; now she in no way avoided
the general conversations which spontaneously
rose out of the life on shipboard, and showed
pleasure in receiving the respectful homage of
several of the men.

A German baron, especially, who was seeking
relief on the ocean from a long-continued
affection of the lungs, hovered about Elise as

much as he dared without its appearing conspicuous. Alfred tried to make himself believe that the encouragement which Elise showed this most charming of her admirers was the welcome sign of growing liking for him. But once when, apparently in anger, he took Elise to task for her marked friendliness, she explained with a smile that all her kindness toward the Baron had no purpose other than to awaken his jealousy and that she was tremendously pleased over the success of her stratagem.

This time Alfred was unable to conceal his impatience, his disappointment any longer. She imagined she had soothed him and given him happiness, but he replied to her confession with words of incomprehensible hardness. In stunned helplessness she listened to them for a while and then suddenly fell unconscious on the deck where the conversation had taken place and had to be carried down into the cabin. The ship's doctor, sufficiently informed by his colleague's letter, did not think a closer examination necessary and gave temporary relief to the tormented heart by the means which already had proved successful. But he could not prevent a repetition of the attacks without any apparent external cause on the following and the third day. Even if morphine never failed in its effect, he could not disguise his fear that the illness might end fatally. He warned Alfred in suitable, but very definite terms, that he must in every way be considerate of his beautiful wife.

In his darkly turbulent anger toward Elise, Alfred would have been quite ready to obey the physician on the one point which was made so emphatic that it was equivalent to a command. But Elise, consumed by desire, as if to appease him by her tenderness, knew how to draw him to her heart again in the lonely hours of the night, no matter how much he resisted. When with half-closed eyes she lay yielding in his arms and he saw on her moist forehead the bluish reflection of the waves which entered through the little cabin-window, he felt a smile rise to his lips from the deepest abysses of his soul. It was only gradually that he recognized it as one of mockery, even of triumph. And as with something like horror he became conscious of his vague hope, he told himself that its fulfillment meant salvation and rescue from all the confusion: Elise. too.

had she been able to see the inevitable end and
been granted a choice, he felt, would have
desired nothing better than to die under his
kisses.   And now when Elise, well aware of the
danger, seemed ready to give herself more and
more passionately and be willing to risk everything for the sake of love and because she
loved, he felt himself strong enough to accept
her sacrifice.   However great it was, it would
bring to a happy solution the destiny of three
human beings whose lives were interwoven in
fateful association.

Night after night he watched the fading light
of her eyes and her dying breath with an expect-
ant fear, and, when a minute later her awakening eyes gleamed gratefully in his and the warm
breath of her lips drank his with new desire, he
felt like one who had been cheated.   All the
deadly insidiousness of his contriving seemed a
useless waste and its effect was merely to fill
Elise's pulses with new and richer life.   And
she was so certain of his love that she
stayed below without the slightest suspicion,
when for hours he kept apart from her during
the day, giving his feverish brow to the cooling
sea-winds on the upper deck.   When he came
back to her with a helpless confused smile, she

answered it with shining eyes as though it were a tender welcome.

At Naples the ship stopped for a day, and then it was to proceed directly to Hamburg without any intermediate stops. Alfred hoped to find here the letter from Adele for which he had pleaded in such urgent words in his last letter from Ceylon. As the sea was rough he did not have to seek an excuse for going ashore without Elise, and entered one of the waiting boats in company with other indifferent travelers. He drove to the post-office, gave his name, and had to leave empty-handed. He tried to reassure himself with the thought that Adele's letter had not been posted in time or had been lost, but he knew from his mood of utter disappointment that any future life without Adele was unthinkable.

As his powers of deception were exhausted his first thought was immediately upon his return to the ship ruthlessly to tell the truth to Elise. But on reflection he soon realized that the consequences of such a confession were inevitable. It would either kill Elise on the spot or drive her into madness or suicide. In either case the reasons for it could hardly remain concealed and might have a disastrous effect upon his relations with Adele. There was the same risk should he postpone his confession until the last moment, until the landing in Hamburg or even the arrival in Vienna.

With his thoughts in a turmoil, Alfred was scarcely any longer aware of their implication. He wandered about on the seashore in the burning sunlight around the noon-hour, until suddenly he felt himself growing dizzy and on the verge of losing consciousness. Frightened, he sank down on a bench and remained seated until the attack relaxed and the mists before his eyes disappeared. He took a breath as if he were just awakening.

Suddenly he knew that in the incomprehensible moment when his consciousness was about to leave him, a horrible decision had definitely matured after long incubation in the depths of his soul. By stealth and cowardice he had for many days sought to bring about the fulfillment of an ardent and cruel wish. Now he had to turn it into action without delay by his own volition, with his own hands. And as if it were the result of long conscious deliberation, a plan leaped complete from his breast.

He rose, and went first into a hotel, where he ate dinner with the best of appetite. Then he

visited three physicians in succession. In each
case he pretended to be a sufferer from excru-
ciating pains, who for years had been accustomed to morphine, but that his supply had
given out. He took the prescriptions for
which he had asked and had them filled in
different pharmacies. When he went aboard
again at sunset, he had in his possession a dose
more than adequate for his purposes.

At the dinner-table on shipboard he enthu-
siastically described an excursion to Pompeii
for which he had used the day to good advantage. He was possessed with an intense
passion for lying; it seemed as though he had to
accentuate a diabolical element in his personal-
ity. He described in elaborate detail a quarter
of an hour he had spent in the Garden of Appius
Claudius, in front of a statuette; actually, of
course, he had never seen it, but merely happened to read about it in a guide-book. Elise
sat beside him, opposite her was the Baron.
The glances of the two met, and Alfred could
not avoid visualizing them as two ghosts that
stared at each other out of empty orbits.

Later, however, as on many a previous
evening, he walked back and forth with Elise
in the moonlight on the upper deck, and the

lights of the coast died out in the distance. When for a second a feeling of weakness overcame him, he reinforced his decision again by imagining that it was Adele's arm which pressed his. This caused a hot wave of passion to run through his veins, and he was convinced that the happiness to come could not be bought too dearly, even at the cost of an atrocious crime. But at the same time something stirred mysteriously in him, something like envy of the young woman by his side, who was destined so soon to find release, painlessly and unsuspectingly, from all of the confusions of life.

When in the cabin he took Elise into his arms for the last time, his mind was so perfectly clear that it was almost unbearable; and yet it was with despairing passion. He felt that he was merely consummating a decree of fate, that his own will no longer had a share in it. Only a touch of his fingers would have been required to overturn the glass, which gleamed bluish on the little table, and the drops of poison would have harmlessly trickled away on the indifferent floor. Alfred lay motionless and waited. He waited until, with his heart standing still, he perceived a familiar gesture of Elise. With half-closed eyes she stretched out her hand for the glass, in order, as always before going to sleep, to quench her thirst.

With his eyelids wide open, motionless, he saw how she raised herself slightly, put the glass to her lips and emptied it with one draught. Then she reclined again with a slight sigh, as was her habit, pillowing her head for sleep on his breast. Alfred heard a slow dull hammering in his temples, heard Elise's even breathing, and heard the waves, as if wailing, strike against the bow of the ship which seemed to glide through time that stood still.

Suddenly he felt a severe tremor running through Elise's body. Both her hands sought for his neck; it seemed as if her fingers wished to bury themselves in his skin; and only then, with a long moan did she open her eyes. Alfred freed himself from her embrace, and leaped out of bed. He saw how she tried to rise, and beat the empty air with her arms. Her look flickered vaguely to and fro in the half-darkness; suddenly she sank back at full length, and remained lying perfectly motionless with short, shallow breathing. Alfred recognized at once that she was absolutely unconscious, and coolly asked himself how long this condition might last before the end would come. At the same time it occurred to him that possibly it was not yet too late to save her. With an obscure desire in this way to tempt destiny once more, he hurried off to call the physician. Either he would himself destroy the fruits of what he had done hitherto, or else by a daring deed find atonement for himself. If the physician recognized what had happened to her, he would count the game as definitely lost; in the other case he would absolve himself from all guilt and remorse for the future.

When Alfred entered the cabin with the physician, they found Elise lying with half-open, glazed eyes, her fingers convulsively clutched in the cover; gleaming drops of perspiration stood out upon her forehead and cheeks. The physician bent down, put his ear to her chest, listened for a long time, shook his head doubtfully, separated Elise's eyelids, held his own hand in front of her lips, and listened again. Then he turned to Alfred and explained that the agony was over. With a distracted look which was not feigned Alfred clasped his hands over his head, sank down in front of the bed, and with forehead pressed against Elise's knee remained lying thus for a short time. Then he turned, and in a dis-

tracted way stared at the physician, who with
a sympathetic look offered him his hand.
Alfred did not take it, and shook his head.
With entire self-possession and clarity of mind
he whispered to himself as with belated self-
reproach, "If we had only followed your
advice." Then in deep sorrow he concealed
his face in his hands. "It is what I might
have thought," he heard the physician reply
with a tone of reproof but yet gently. With
an overwhelming feeling of triumph he was
conscious of a glowing light in his eyes behind
his twitching lids.

On the following day, as demanded by the
regulations, Elise's body was let down into the
sea. As a widower, Alfred felt himself surrounded by a general though silent and re-
served sympathy. No one dared to disturb
him when he walked back and forth on the
deck for hours and looked into the distance.
No one would have suspected that for him it
was filled with the fragrance of extravagant
hopes.

The Baron alone sometimes joined him for a
few short minutes as he walked to and fro, and
it was obvious that he intentionally avoided
any mention of the death. Alfred knew very

well that the Baron's only motive in joining
him was because he wanted to feel for a few
minutes the atmosphere of the dead woman he
had so loved. These minutes were the only
ones for Alfred when he felt himself touched
by the past; otherwise he put himself entirely
above his act, and what it might mean to
human beings. In the living present the
image of her whom he so desired, whom he had
gained by his guilt, rose before him. When he
looked down upon the water from the bow of
the ship, it seemed to him as if he saw her glid-
ing peacefully over buried worlds which lay in
deep sleep and were indifferent whether they
had sunken out of sight yesterday or a thousand years ago.

It was not until they were within sight of the
German coast that his pulses beat faster. It
was his intention to stay in Hamburg no longer
than was necessary to get the letter which
should be waiting for him there; then he meant
to set out for home by the next train. The
wearisome delay of disembarkation filled him
with torturing impatience. He breathed a
sigh of relief when his luggage was at last on a
carriage and he drove toward the post-office
through the streets of the city over which the

late spring afternoon hung with tiny pink
clouds. He handed his card to the clerk, and
with burning eyes watched him run through the
letters. He held out his hand expectantly, and
received the answer that there was nothing for
him, neither letter, nor card, nor telegram.
He smiled incredulously, and, in an almost
humble tone of voice of which he was immediately ashamed, he asked the clerk to look again.
And now Alfred tried to decipher the addresses
beneath the edges of the envelopes. Again and
again he seemed to recognize his name in
Adele's handwriting; several times he had
already hopefully extended his hands, only to
be told again that he was mistaken. Finally
the clerk put the package back in its compartment, shook his head, and turned away.

Alfred thanked him with exaggerated polite-
ness, and a minute later stood half-stupefied
before the entrance. One thing alone was
clear to him. For the time being he had to
stay here, as it was impossible for him to go on
to Vienna without some word from Adele in his
possession. He drove to a hotel, engaged a
room, and first of all wrote the following words
on one of the telegram blanks: "No word
from you. Incomprehensible. Much dis-

turbed. Home the day after to-morrow. When
can I see you? Answer at once." He added
the address, and handed in the message with
reply prepaid.

When he entered the lobby where the evening lights were already burning, he felt two eyes
fixed upon him.   From an armchair, with a
newspaper across his knees, seriously, without
rising, the Baron greeted him, He had only
hurriedly said good-by to him on shipboard.
Alfred appeared to be pleased at the unexpected meeting, and even believed that he
actually was. He informed the Baron of his
intention to stay over until to-morrow.
In spite of the pallor of his cheeks and his continuous slight cough, the Baron insisted that he
was feeling very well. During dinner he sug-
gested that they hunt up a vaudeville. When
Alfred hesitated, he remarked gently and with
lowered lashes that grief had never yet brought
back any one from the dead. Alfred laughed,
and was startled by his laughter. He imagined
that the Baron had noticed his embarrassment,
and felt immediately that the wisest thing for
him to do would be to join the Baron.

Soon afterwards he sat with him in a box,
drinking champagne. Through the smoke and

fumes he saw gymnasts and clowns exhibit
their arts and tricks to the cheap sounds of a
strident orchestra. He heard half-naked
women sing impudent songs, and, as if under
some mad compulsion, called the attention of
his silent companion to the shapely legs and
opulent bosoms that were displayed on the
stage. He joked with a flower-girl, and threw
a yellow rose at the feet of one of the dancers
who seductively shook her black curls. He
laughed aloud when he saw the thin lips of the
Baron twitch as if with bitterness and disgust.
Later it seemed to him as if hundreds on the
floor below were looking at him with malignant
curiosity, and as if all the whispering and
buzzing were solely on his account. A chilling
fear crept up and down his back; then he
remembered that he had emptied several
glasses of champagne in too rapid succession,
and he felt calm again.

He was pleased to note that while he had
leaned over the edge of the box, two rouged
women had drawn the Baron into conversation;
he breathed with relief as if he had escaped a
danger, rose, and nodded to his companion as if
to encourage and wish him good luck in his
adventure. Soon he was walking alone through

streets he had never before seen and would
never see again. He was whistling some sort
of melody to himself. He had the feeling that
he was wandering in a dream city, and in the
cool night air finally managed to get back to
his hotel.

When he awoke in the morning after a heavy,
deep sleep, he first had to collect his wits to
remember that he was no longer on shipboard
and that the white gleaming thing was not
Elise's morning-gown but a window-curtain.
With an immense effort of the will he repelled
the tide of memory which rose threateningly
within him, and rang. Along with breakfast
a telegram was also brought him. He left it
lying on the tray, as long as the waiter remained in the room; he thought that his self-
control deserved some sort of reward.

The door had hardly closed before he opened
the telegram with trembling fingers. At first
the letters dissolved before his eyes, but suddenly they stood rigid and gigantic: "To-
morrow, eleven o'clock. Adele." He ran
hither and thither, laughed between his teeth,
and did not let himself be chilled by the abrupt
cold tone of the summons. It was her way.
Even if he didn't find everything at home as

he had hoped a little while ago, even if disagreeable revelations were in store for him, what would that signify? He would stand facing her again, in the light of her eyes, in the fragrance of her breath. The monstrous thing he had done would not have been in vain.

It was impossible for him to stay in the hotel any longer. For the short period of time until the departure of his train, he ran about the city with his eyelids abnormally open, but without seeing men or objects. At noon he left Hamburg, and stared for hours and hours through the panes upon the flying landscape. He repressed with his well-tried will-power everything in the way of thoughts, hopes, and fears that sought to stir within him. Whenever, so as not to appear conspicuous to his fellow travelers, he took up a newspaper or book, he counted without reading, over and over again, to one hundred, five hundred, a thousand.

When night fell the consuming intensity of his desire broke through all his efforts at remaining calm. He called himself foolish for having misconstrued the lack of news from her and the tone of the last message. He could find nothing with which to reproach Adele, except that she had adhered more honestly to the agreement than he. But if in some way she should have discovered that he had traveled with a woman companion, he felt his love strong enough to win her back against jealousy, bitterness, or any feeling of affront. He had made himself so much a master of his wakeful dreams, that he was able, in this endless night, to hear the melody of her voice and to see the outlines of her figure and face; he even felt her kiss, more consumingly dear than ever reality had brought it to him from her lips.

He was home. With friendly comfort his house received him. He enjoyed the carefully prepared breakfast. For the first time in many days, it seemed to him, he was able to think again with perfect composure of the other one, the one that slept in the silent sea, freed for all time from every earthly sorrow. For a moment it even seemed to him as if the succession of hours from the landing in Naples until Elise's death was merely a figment of his shattered nerves, and as if the fatal ending had come naturally in the course of the disease quite as the physicians had anticipated and even foretold.

The man who in a sunlit foreign city had craftily hastened from physician to physician and from chemist to chemist and with cruel calculation had collected the deadly poison and also the man who with wanton pleasure had folded his beloved in his arms an hour before he was about to send her into the beyond, seemed to him quite another person from the one who sat here between these familiar walls in unchanged, comfortable, middle-class surroundings, drinking his tea. It seemed that the other was a some one greater than he, to whom he himself had to look up with trembling admiration. But later, when he had finished his bath and his mirror showed him his slender, naked image, he was suddenly aware that nevertheless it was he himself who had done the incomprehensible thing. He saw his eyes shine with a hard gleam; he felt himself more worthy than ever of clasping the waiting bride to his heart, and with an expression of mocking superiority on his lips he felt surer of her love than ever before.

At the appointed hour he entered the yellow reception-room, which he had left on almost the same day a year ago. In a minute Adele stood before him, unconstrained, as if she had taken leave of him the day before; she held out her hand, and let it linger in his clasp for a long

kiss. What is keeping me from embracing
her, he asked himself. Then he heard her
talking with her dark voice, that voice which
he had heard in his dreams only last night.
He became aware that he himself had not yet
spoken a word; he had merely whispered her
name when she had appeared before him.

She hoped, she began, that he would not be
offended because she had not answered his
beautiful letters; it happened to be a fact that
certain matters can be better and more simply
disposed of face to face than by letter. Her
silence surely must have prepared him for
the fact that there had been many changes,
and the cold tone of her telegram, as she
was quite ready to confess, had been entirely
intentional. For about half a year she had
been engaged to some one else. And she
mentioned a name which Alfred knew. It
was that of one of the many good friends
of former days to whom he had given so
little thought during the course of the past
year, as, indeed, he had to most of the people
he had known in the past. He listened quietly
to Adele, stared fixedly at her smooth brow
and then beyond her into the void, and in
his ears there was a sound as of distant waves.

surging over sunken worlds. Suddenly he
saw something like a gleam of fear light in
Adele's eyes. He knew that he stood opposite
her, pale as death, with a terrifying look.
Before he knew it, he said with a hard, toneless
voice: "That won't do, Adele, you are mistaken, you dare not."

That he had at last found words, apparently
reassured her. She smiled again in her polite
way and explained, that it was not she, but
he who was mistaken. She did dare to, she
dared anything she wanted. She hadn't even
been engaged to him; they had parted as free
human beings, without any obligations, she
as well as he. And since she no longer loved
him, but the other one, the whole matter was
settled. He must see that and adapt himself.
Otherwise she really would have to regret not
having followed her father's advice of this
morning, which was simply no longer to be
at home to Alfred. And she sat opposite him
with clear, distant eyes, the slender hands
entwined over her knee.

Alfred felt that it required his entire self-
control not to do something ridiculous or
horrible. He wasn't clear about what he
really wanted, whether to fling himself upon

her neck and strangle her, or to throw himself
on the floor and cry like a child. But of what
use was it to think about it. He had no
choice and already lay as if struck down;
he had just presence of mind enough to seize
Adele's hands, as she was about to hurry
away, and look up and plead with her that she
stay. Only a quarter of an hour! To listen
to him! Surely he could ask that of her,
after all that had been between them. He
had so much to tell her, more than she could
imagine, and she was in duty bound to listen
to it. For if she knew everything, then she
would also know, that he belonged to her and
she to him; know that she could not belong
to any other, that he had won her for himself
in sin and torment; that before his great
right to her all others were as dust, deep dust.
She was joined to him, indissolubly, for all
eternity, as was he to her. On his knees
before her, convulsively clasping her hands
in his, his eyes fixed in hers, he let his words
flow. He told her all the events of the past
year; told how he had loved another before
her, and how he had set out on a journey with
that other one who was ill and had no one in
the world beside him: how he had consumed

himself in the torments of longing, but how
the other one, helpless and clinging, had
twined around his neck. He told how when
he had come to the limit of his pain he had
pityingly and craftily poisoned the other because of his love for *her*, *her*, whose hands he
held in his with a love the like of which had
never been seen on earth. The other one had
neither desired nor been able to live without
him, and he had freed her from the bonds of
this life. The poor thing now slept beneath
distant ocean waves. She was a sacrifice for
a happiness without equal, just as the price
by which he had won it was without equal.

Adele had left him her hands; nor did she
release her look from his. She listened to
what he was telling her, and he didn't just
know how. Did it seem to her a fairy-tale
about strange alien creatures or a newspaper
report about people that didn't concern her?
Perhaps, she didn't even believe what he was
telling her. But, at any rate, it was a matter
of indifference to her whether truth or untruth
fell from his lips. He felt his powerlessness
before her more and more. He saw all his
words glide empty and cool down her sides;
and finally, when he wanted to read his fate

upon her lips, which he knew beforehand, she merely shook her head. He looked at her with anguish, knowing and yet uncertain, with a confused question in his flickering eyes.

"No," she said unbendingly, "all is over."

And he knew that with this "no" everything was at an end forever. Adele's expression remained entirely unmoved. It did not betray the slightest memory of the tenderness that had been, not even of aversion, nothing but an annihilating look of indifference and boredom.

Alfred bowed his head with an empty smile as if of understanding. He no longer held her hands which absent-mindedly she let hang down, and he turned and left. The door remained open behind him, and he felt a cold breath of air on his neck. As he went down the stairs he knew there was nothing left for him to do but to end it all. This decision was irrevocable. He walked home slowly and idly through the caressing spring day, as to a much-desired sleep after a night of debauch.

In his room somebody was waiting for him. It was the Baron. Without taking the hand which Alfred held out, he declared that he only desired a few words with him. On Alfred's short, courteous nod he continued: "I feel it necessary to tell you that I consider you a scoundrel." Very good, thought Alfred, there is no objection to this conclusion, and he replied calmly, "I am at your service. To-morrow morning, if it's satisfactory." The Baron shook his head abruptly. It appeared that already on shipboard he had carefully laid his plans.

Two young men from the German Embassy were waiting for his further directions. He expressed the hope that since this was his opponent's home he would find no difficulty in having the matter arranged before evening. Alfred thought he could promise this. For a moment he had the impulse to confess the whole truth to the Baron, but the immense hatred that radiated from his cold brow made him fear, that, while he might now perhaps suspect the truth, he would then turn him over to the courts. So he chose to remain silent.

Alfred found the men he required without difficulty. One was Adele's fiancé, the other a young officer with whom he had spent many a gay day in the past. Before sunset he stood opposite the Baron in the meadows near the Danube, a favorite haunt for meetings like this. A peace which seemed like happiness filled him after the turmoil of the days that had just passed. When he saw the barrel of the pistol aimed at him, during the three seconds, counted off by a distant voice and falling like three cold drops from the evening sky upon the ringing ground, he thought of the woman he loved so infinitely over whose decaying body the waves of the ocean ran. And as he lay on the ground and something dark bent down over him, held him close, and refused to let go of him again, he felt happy, that this was expiation for her, that he was vanishing toward her into the nothing which he had so long desired.

THE BLIND GERONIMO AND
HIS BROTHER

THE BLIND GERONIMO AND
HIS BROTHER

THE blind Geronimo rose from the bench and took up his guitar, which lay in readiness on the table beside the wineglass. He had heard the distant rumbling of the first carriage. Now he felt his familiar way toward the open door, and then went down the narrow wooden stairs which led to the covered courtyard. His brother followed him, and both took their position close by the stairs with their backs to the wall so as to be protected against the damp cold wind which swept over the soggy ground through the open gates.

All the carriages that went by the way of the Stelvio Pass had to pass beneath the gloomy archway of the old inn. For travelers going from Italy to Tyrol, it was the last stopping-place before the summit. It didn't invite to a long stay, for the road here ran rather level, without views, between barren

elevations. The blind Italian and his brother
Carlo practically made their home here during
the summer months.

The post-coach drove in; other vehicles
soon followed it. Most of the travelers kept
their seats, well wrapped in plaids and cloaks;
others alighted and impatiently walked back
and forth between the gates. The weather
grew worse, a cold rain fell. After a succession of beautiful days it seemed as if autumn
had broken suddenly and all too soon.

The blind man sang and accompanied himself on his guitar; he sang with an uneven
voice, which sometimes suddenly became
shrill as always when he had been drinking.
From time to time he turned his head upward
with an expression of fruitless pleading. Yet
the lines of his face, with its black stubble of
beard and its bluish lips, remained completely
immobile. His older brother stood beside him,
almost motionless. When some one dropped
a coin in his hat, he nodded his thanks,
and looked into the giver's face with a quick,
almost wandering glance. But immediately,
almost timidly, he looked away again, and
stared, like his brother, into the void. It was

as if his eyes were ashamed of the light which
was granted to them, but of which they could
not give a single ray to the blind brother.

"Bring me some wine," said Geronimo,
and Carlo went, obedient as always. As he
ascended the stairs, Geronimo began to sing
again. He had long since ceased listening to
his own voice, and so he could pay attention
to what was going on in his neighborhood.
Just now he heard two whispering voices
quite close by, those of a young man and a
young woman. He wondered how often these
two might have gone back and forth over the
same way, for, in his blindness and intoxication,
it sometimes seemed as if day after day the
same people wandered over the pass, now
from the north to the south, now from the
south to the north. And so it seemed he had
known this young couple for a long time.

Carlo came down and handed Geronimo a
glass of wine. The blind man raised his glass
to the young couple and said, "To your
health, friends."

"Thanks!" said the young man, but the
young woman drew him away, for the blind
man made her feel uncomfortable.

Now a carriage with a rather noisy company drove in — father, mother, three children, a nurse.

"German family," said Geronimo in a low voice to Carlo.

The father gave a piece of money to each of the children, and each one was permitted to toss it into the hat of the beggar. Every time Geronimo inclined his head in thanks. The oldest boy peered with timid curiosity into the beggar's face. Carlo watched the boy. As always when he saw such children he had to think of the fact that Geronimo was just at that age when the accident occurred which had cost him his sight. He even to-day, after almost twenty years, remembered the day with perfect clarity. His ears still rang with the shrill childish cry with which the little Geronimo had dropped on the grass; he still saw the sun play in circles upon the white garden-wall and heard the Sunday bells which had sounded at that moment.

As on many an occasion, he had aimed at the ash-tree near the wall, and when he heard the cry he imagined at once that he had wounded his little brother who had just run past. He let the blowgun slip from his hands,

leaped through the window into the garden,
and dashed toward his little brother who lay
on the grass, wailing, with his hands clasped
to his face. Blood was flowing down along
his right cheek and neck. At this very moment
their father came home from the fields through
the little garden-gate, and now both knelt
down beside the crying child without knowing
what to do. Neighbors hurried hither; the
old Vanetti woman was the first who succeeded in withdrawing the child's hands from
his face. Then the blacksmith, to whom
Carlo was apprenticed, came along too. He
had some slight knowledge of surgery, and
saw immediately that the right eye was lost.
The physician who came from Poschiavo in
the evening also could not do anything further.
He indicated that the other eye was likewise
endangered. And so it turned out. A year later
the world turned into night for Geronimo. At
first they tried to persuade him that he could
be cured later, and he seemed to believe it.

Carlo, who knew the truth, wandered aimlessly over the highway for many days and
nights, among the vineyards and forests, and
was on the verge of killing himself. The
priest in whom he confided explained that it

was his duty to live and to devote his life to
his brother. A great pity seized him. It was
only when he was with the blind boy, when he
stroked his hair, kissed his forehead, told him
stories, led him about in the fields behind the
house and among the vine-trellises, that his
unhappiness was less poignant.

Quite at the beginning he had neglected his
hours at the blacksmith shop, because he
did not want to be separated from his brother;
later he could not make up his mind to take
up his trade again, though his father urged
him and was troubled. One day Carlo noticed
that Geronimo no longer talked about his
misfortune. Soon he knew why. The blind
boy had come to understand that he would
never again see the sky, the hills, the streets,
people, light. Now Carlo's unhappiness was
greater than ever, though he tried to reassure
himself with the thought that the accident
was entirely unintentional on his part.

And sometimes, when early in the morning
he watched his brother, lying beside him, he
was mortally afraid of seeing him wake up.
He then ran out into the garden, so that he
might not be present when the dead eyes
each day anew seemed to seek the light which

had gone out for them forever. It was at this time that it occurred to Carlo to have Geronimo take up music, for he had a pleasing voice. The schoolmaster of Tola, who sometimes came on Sundays, taught him to play on the guitar. The blind boy then did not dream that this new art was once to serve him as a means of livelihood.

With that sad summer's day misfortune seemed permanently to have settled in old Lagardi's house. The harvest failed year after year, and the old man was cheated by relatives of the small sum of money he had saved. When on a sultry August day he fell down in the open field under a stroke of apoplexy and died, he left nothing but debts. The little property was sold; the two brothers were poor and without shelter, and left the village.

Carlo was twenty years old, Geronimo fifteen. It was then that the wandering beggar's existence which still was theirs began. At first Carlo had thought of finding some sort of work which might support both him and his brother, but success would not come. Besides, Geronimo was restless everywhere; he always wanted to be moving.

It was twenty years now that they had

wandered about among the roads and passes, in Northern Italy and Southern Tyrol, always where the densest crowd of travelers went by.

And even if after so many years Carlo no longer felt the burning torment with which formerly every gleam of the sun, every view of a friendly landscape, had filled him, there was still a continuous pity in him, persistent and unconscious, like the beat of his heart and his breath. And he was glad when Geronimo got drunk.

The carriage with the German family had driven away. Carlo sat down, as was his favorite habit, on the lowest step of the stairs, but Geronimo remained standing; he let his arms hang down limply and kept his head turned upward.

Maria, the maid, came out of the main room of the inn.

"Get much to-day?" she called down to them.

Carlo did not even turn around. The blind man bent down to his glass, raised it from the ground, and held it out toward Maria. Sometimes in the evening she sat by his side in the inn; he knew, too, that she was beautiful.

Carlo bent forward, and looked out toward

the road.   The wind blew and the rain rattled,
so that the rumble of the approaching carriage
was drowned out by the noisy sounds.   Carlo
rose and again took his place by his brother's
side.

Geronimo began to sing, just as soon as the
carriage entered the gate; there was only a
single passenger.   The driver quickly unhar-
nessed the horses, and then hurried up into the
inn.   For a while the traveler remained sitting
in his corner, completely wrapped up in a gray
raincoat; he seemed entirely oblivious to the
song.   After a while he leapt from the carriage
and walked hurriedly to and fro, without moving very far away from the carriage.   He rubbed
his hands together all the time to warm himself.
Only now did he seem to notice the beggars.
He stood still, facing them, and for a long time
looked critically at them.   Carlo inclined his
head slightly, as if in greeting.   The traveler
was a very young man, with an attractive,
beardless face and restless eyes.   After he had
stood before the beggars for a considerable
time, he hastened to the gateway again,
through which he was to continue his journey,
and shook his head in annoyance at the cheer-
less prospect of rain and fog.

"Well?" asked Geronimo.

"Nothing yet," replied Carlo. "He will probably give something when he leaves."

The traveler came back again and leaned against the pole of the carriage. The blind man began to sing. Now the young man suddenly seemed to listen with great interest. The hostler appeared, and harnessed the horses again. And only now, as if just remembering it, the young man went down into his pocket, and gave Carlo a franc.

"Oh, thank you, thank you," said he.

The traveler took his seat in the carriage, and again wrapped himself up in his cloak. Carlo picked up the glass from the ground, and went up the wooden stairs. The traveler leaned out beyond the carriage, and shook his head with an expression of simultaneous superiority and sadness. Suddenly a fancy took him, and he smiled. He said to the blind man, who stood scarcely two paces away: "What is your name?"

"Geronimo."

"Well, Geronimo, don't let them cheat you." At this moment the coachman appeared at the topmost step.

"How so, sir, cheat?"

"I gave your companion a twenty-franc piece."

"Oh, sir, thank you, thank you!"

"Very well; but look out."

"He is my brother, sir; he wouldn't cheat me."

The young man hesitated for a moment, but while he was still pondering, the driver had gotten on his seat and started the horses. The young man leaned back with a movement of the head, as if he meant to say, "Fate, take your course!" and the carriage drove off.

The blind man expressed his thanks with lively gestures of both hands as the carriage drove off. Now he heard Carlo, who was just coming out of the inn. He called down to him: "Come, Geronimo, it's warm up here; Maria has built a fire."

Geronimo nodded, took his guitar, and felt his way along the banister up the steps. Still on the stairs he called out: "Let me touch it. It is a long time since I have touched a gold piece."

"What's the matter?" asked Carlo. "What are you talking about?"

Geronimo was upstairs, and felt with both hands for his brother's head, a gesture with which he was always in the habit of expressing joy or tenderness. "Carlo, dear brother, there still are good people."

"Of course," said Carlo. "We got two lire and thirty centisimi so far, and here is some Austrian money, perhaps half a lire."

"And twenty francs—and twenty francs," cried Geronimo. "I know about them!" He stumbled into the room, and sat down heavily on a bench.

"You know about what?" asked Carlo.

"No joking! Put it in my hand! It is so long since I have held a gold piece in my hand."

"What do you want? Where am I to get a gold piece from? There are two or three lire."

The blind man struck the table. "Enough of that now, enough! Are you trying to hide something from me?"

Carlo looked at his brother with apprehension and surprise. He sat down beside him, moved quite close, and touched his arm appeasingly. "I am hiding nothing from you. How could you imagine I would? No one ever thought of giving me a gold piece."

"But he told me so!"

"Who?"

"The young man, who walked back and forth."

"Who? I don't understand you!"

"He said to me, 'What is your name?' and then, 'Look out, look out, don't let them cheat you.' "

"You must have dreamed it, Geronimo—it is pure nonsense!"

"Nonsense? I heard it, and my hearing is good. 'Don't let them cheat you, I gave him a gold piece . . . '—no, he said, 'I gave him a twenty-franc piece.' "

The tavern-keeper entered. "Well, what's the matter with you? Have you given up business? A coach with four horses has just driven up."

"Come!" exclaimed Carlo, "Come!"

Geronimo kept his seat. "But why? Why should I come? What's the use? You stand there and——"

Carlo touched his arm. "Hush, now, come down!"

Geronimo was silent, and obeyed his brother. But on the steps he said: "We are not through talking yet, not yet!"

Carlo did not understand what had happened. Had Geronimo suddenly gone mad?

For, even if he did easily fly into a passion, he had never spoken in the manner he had now.

Two Englishmen sat in the carriage that had just arrived. Carlo raised his hat, and the blind man sang. One of the Englishmen had left the carriage and tossed a couple of coins into Carlo's hat. Carlo said, "Thank you," and then as if to himself, "Twenty centisimi!" Geronimo's face remained unmoved; he began a new song. The carriage with the two Englishmen drove away.

The brothers ascended the stairs in silence. Geronimo sat down on the bench, Carlo remained standing by the stove.

"Why don't you say something?" asked Geronimo.

"Well," replied Carlo, "it happened just as I have told you." His voice trembled a little.

"What did you say?" asked Geronimo.

"Perhaps he was crazy."

"Crazy? Fine! If some one says, 'I have given your brother twenty francs,' then he is crazy—eh, and why did he say, 'Don't let them cheat you'—eh?"

"Maybe he wasn't crazy . . . but there are people who like to play jokes on poor people . . . "

"Eh!" screamed Geronimo. "Jokes? Of course, you had to say that—I was waiting for it!" He emptied the glass of wine before him.

"But, Geronimo!" Carlo exclaimed, and in his consternation he felt barely able to speak, "why should I . . . how can you imagine. . .?"

"Why does your voice tremble . . . eh? . . . why?"

"Geronimo, I swear, I——"

"Eh—and I don't believe you! You are laughing now . . . I know you are laughing now."

The hostler from below called, "Hello, blind man, there are people here."

Entirely mechanically, the brothers rose, and went down the stairs. Two carriages had arrived together, one with three men and the other with an old married couple. Geronimo sang; Carlo stood beside him, disconcerted. What was he to do? His brother did not believe him. How was that possible? And he looked with an anxious, sidewise glance at Geronimo, who sang his songs with a cracked voice. It seemed to him as if he saw thoughts flit across his brow, which he had never before noticed.

The carriages had already left, but Geronimo

went on singing. Carlo did not dare to interrupt him. He did not know what to say; he
was afraid his voice would tremble again.
Then laughter sounded from above, and Maria
called out, "What are you still singing for?
You won't get nothing from me!"

Geronimo stopped in the middle of a melody;
it sounded as if his voice and the strings had
broken at the same moment. Then he went
up the steps again, and Carlo followed him.
In the inn he sat down beside him. What was
he to do? There was nothing else, but to
try again to enlighten his brother.

"Geronimo," he said, "I swear to you . . .
think, Geronimo, how can you believe that
I——"

Geronimo remained silent; his dead eyes
seemed to look out through the window into
the gray mist.   Carlo continued speaking,
"Well, maybe he wasn't just crazy, he may
have been mistaken . . . yes, he was mistaken. . . . " But he felt that he himself
didn't believe what he was saying.

Geronimo impatiently moved away, but
Carlo went on talking, with sudden animation:
"Why should I—you know I don't eat or
drink any more than you, and when I buy

myself a new coat, you know that too. What
use would I have for so much money? What
should I do with it?"

Then Geronimo ejaculated between his teeth,
"Don't lie, I hear how you lie!"

"I am not lying, Geronimo, I am not lying!"
said Carlo, frightened.

"Eh! You've given it to her already? Or
will she get it later?" screamed Geronimo.

"Maria?"

"Who else, but Maria? Eh, you liar, you
thief!" And as if he no longer wished to sit
beside him at the table, he shoved his brother
in the ribs with the elbow.

Carlo got up. At first he stared at his
brother; then he left the room, and went by
the stairway into the courtyard. With wide-
open eyes he looked out upon the highway,
which disappeared before him in a brownish
fog. The rain had stopped. Carlo thrust his
hands in his trousers' pockets, and went out
into the open. He felt as if his brother had
driven him away. What in the world had
happened? He couldn't yet grasp it. What
sort of a person had it been? He had given a
single franc, and said it was twenty! He must
have had some reason. And Carlo searched

his memory, as to whether somewhere he had made an enemy and he had sent the stranger to avenge himself. . . . But as far back as he could remember, he had never given an affront to any one, had never had a serious quarrel with any one. For twenty years he had never done anything but stand in courtyards or on the edge of the roads with hat in hand . . . Was, perhaps, some one angry with him on a woman's account? . . . But what a long time since he had had anything to do with a woman. . . . The waitress in La Rosa had been the last one, the spring before . . . but surely no one envied him on her account. . . . He couldn't understand it at all! . . . What sort of people might there be out in that world which he didn't know? . . . They came from everywhere. . . . What did he know of them? . . . This stranger must have had some motive that made him say, 'I have given your brother twenty francs.' . . . Surely . . . But what was he to do now? . . . It had suddenly become obvious, that Geronimo distrusted him! . . . He could not bear this! He had to do something to counteract it. . . . . And he hurried back.

When he again entered the room of the inn, Geronimo lay stretched out on the bench and seemed not to notice Carlo's entrance. Maria brought food and drink for the two. They didn't exchange a word during the meal. When Maria was clearing away the plates, Geronimo suddenly laughed out aloud and said to her, "What are you going to buy yourself with it?"

"With what?"

"Well, what? A new skirt or earrings?"

"What does he want of me?" she said, turning to Carlo.

In the meantime there was the sound of heavy-laden vehicles down in the courtyard, loud voices were heard, and Maria hurried down. After a few minutes three drivers entered, and sat down at the table; the innkeeper went up to them and greeted them. They growled about the bad weather.

"You are going to have snow to-night," said one of them.

The second one told how, ten years ago in the middle of August, he had been snowed in in the pass, and had almost been frozen to death. Maria sat down with them. The hostler also joined them, and asked about his parents who lived down in Bormio.

Now another carriage with travelers arrived. Geronimo and Carlo went down: Geronimo sang. Carlo held out his hat, and the travelers gave their alms. Geronimo seemed perfectly quiet now. Sometimes he asked, "How much?" and inclined his head slightly at Carlo's replies. In the meantime Carlo tried to put his thoughts in order. But he always had a dead feeling that something terrible had happened, and that he was entirely defenseless.

When the brothers again went up the stairs, they heard the confused talk and the laughter of the drivers above. The youngest called out to Geronimo, "Sing something for us, we'll pay!—Won't we?" He turned toward the others.

Maria, who was just coming with a bottle of red wine, said, "Don't start anything to-day; he is in a bad humor."

Instead of answering, Geronimo stood up in the centre of the room, and began to sing. When he stopped, the drivers clapped their hands.

"Come here, Carlo," called one of them, "we want to throw our money into the hat like the people below!" And he took a small coin and held up his hand, as if to drop it in the hat which Carlo held out. Then the blind man sought to lay hold of the driver's arm and said,

"Rather me, rather me! It might miss—fall down beside it!"

"How so, beside it?"

"Eh, maybe! Between Maria's legs!"

Everybody laughed, the innkeeper and Maria too; Carlo alone stood there motionless. Never before had Geronimo joked in that way!

"Sit down with us," the drivers exclaimed. "You are a gay bird!" And they moved closer together to make room for Geronimo. They talked more loudly and confusedly; Geronimo joined in, more loudly and gayer than usual, and didn't stop drinking. When Maria came in again, he tried to pull her over his way. One of the drivers said, laughing, "Do you think she's beautiful? She is an ugly old woman!"

The blind man, however, drew Maria down on his lap. "You are all blockheads," he said. "Do you think I need my eyes to see? I know too where Carlo is now—eh?—he's standing over there by the stove with his hands in his trousers' pockets, and laughs."

They all looked at Carlo, who leaned with open mouth against the stove and now actually screwed his face into a grin, as if he did not dare to give his brother the lie.

The hostler came in. If the drivers wanted
to reach Bormio before nightfall, they would
have to hurry. They got up, and took a noisy
leave. The two brothers again were alone in
the room. It was the hour around which they
sometimes were in the habit of sleeping. As
always about this time, the hours of early
afternoon, quiet fell over the inn. Geronimo
with his head on the table, seemed to sleep.
Carlo, at first, walked back and forth; then he
sat down on the bench. He was very tired.
It seemed to him as if he were involved in a
bad dream. He had to think of all sorts of
things, of yesterday, the day before yesterday,
and all the days that had been, and especially
of the warm summer days and the white high-
ways over which he and his brother were accustomed to wander. Everything seemed so
far away and incomprehensible, as if it could
never be thus again.

Late in the afternoon the mail coach from
Tyrol arrived, and soon afterwards at brief
intervals carriages also, bound southward.
Four more times the brothers had to go down
into the courtyard. When they ascended the
last time dusk had fallen, and the little oil
lamp which hung down from the wooden ceiling

sputtered. Laborers came. They were em-
ployed in a nearby quarry, and had put up
their wooden shacks a couple of hundred paces
below the inn. Geronimo sat down with them;
Carlo remained by himself at his table. It
seemed to him as if his solitude had lasted a
very long time already.

He heard Geronimo across the way telling
about his childhood, loudly, almost shrilly;
that he still remembered very well all sorts of
things which he had seen with his own eyes,
persons and objects; that he recalled his father
who worked in the fields, the little garden with
the ash-tree by the wall, the low house belonging to them, the two little daughters of the
shoemaker, the vineyard behind the church,
yes, even his own childish face as it had looked
at him out of the mirror. How many a time
Carlo had heard all this! To-day he could not
bear it. It had a different sound from other
times; every word that Geronimo spoke ac-
quired a new meaning and seemed to be
directed at him.

He slipped out, and again went to the highway which now lay in complete darkness.
The rain had ceased, the air was very chill, and
an almost luring thought came to Carlo to go

on and on deep into the darkness; finally to lie
down somewhere in a roadside ditch, to fall
asleep, never to awake again.

Suddenly he heard the rumbling of a carriage, and saw the glimmering light of two
lanterns, approaching closer and closer. Two
men sat in the carriage which drove by. One
of them, with a narrow, beardless face, started
with fright when, under the lantern light,
Carlo's figure rose out of the darkness. Carlo,
who had remained standing still, raised his hat.
The carriage and the lights disappeared. Carlo
again stood deep in the darkness. Suddenly
he started. For the first time in his life the
darkness frightened him. He felt as if he could
not bear it another minute. In a strange way
the terrors which he himself felt mingled in his
dulled senses with a tormenting pity for his
blind brother, and they drove him home.

When he entered the inn, he saw the two
travelers that had driven past him sitting at a
table with a bottle of red wine, conversing
earnestly with each other. They hardly looked
up when he entered.

At the other table Geronimo sat as before
with the laborers.

"Where have you been, Carlo?" said the

innkeeper to him at the door. "Why do you leave your brother alone?"

"What is the trouble?" asked Carlo, frightened.

"Geronimo is treating the people. It's all the same to me, but you should remember that hard times will soon be with us again."

Carlo quickly went up to his brother, and took hold of his arm. "Come!" he said.

"What do you want?" screamed Geronimo.

"Come to bed," said Carlo.

"Leave me alone, leave me alone! *I* earn the money, I can do with my money what I please—eh!—you can't pocket all of it! You think he gives all of it to me! Oh no! I am only a blind man! But there are people— there are people who say to me, 'I have given your brother twenty francs!' "

The laborers laughed.

"That's enough now," said Carlo, "come!" And he pulled his brother with him, almost dragged him up the stairs to the barren garret where they had their couch. Along the whole way Geronimo screamed, "Yes, now it's come to light, now I know! Ah, just wait! Where is she? Where is Maria? Or are you putting it in bank for her?—Eh, I sing for you, I play the guitar, you live off me—and you are a thief." He fell down on the straw mattress.

A pallid glimmer of light entered from the hallway; on the other side, the door of the only guest-room in the inn stood open, and Maria was getting the beds ready for the night. Carlo stood in front of his brother, and saw him lying there with bloated face, bluish lips, the damp hair sticking to his forehead, looking many years older than he was. And slowly he began to understand. The blind man's suspicion was not a thing of to-day; it must have lain dormant in him, and only the occasion, or, perhaps, the courage had lacked for him to express it openly.

And all that Carlo had done for him had been in vain; vain was his penance, vain the sacrifice of his entire life. What was he to do now? Should he continue day after day, for who knows how much longer, to lead him through his eternal night, watch over him, beg for him, and have no other reward but distrust and curses? If his brother considered him a thief, a stranger would do as well as he, or even better. Truly, it would be wisest to leave him alone, and separate permanently. Then Geronimo would perceive how unjust he had been, then he would really learn what it means to be cheated and robbed, be alone and miserable. And as for himself, what was he to do? Well, he wasn't exactly old yet; if he were by himself alone, there were all sorts of things he could do. As a hostler at any rate he could always earn his keep anywhere.

But while these thoughts went through his head, his eyes remained fixed on his brother. And suddenly he visualized him sitting alone on a stone at the edge of a sunlit street, staring with his wide-open, white eyes toward heaven, which could not blind him, and grasping with his hands into the night which always surrounded him. And he felt that just as the blind man had no one in the world but him, so too he had no one beside his brother. He knew that his love for this brother completely filled his life, and he knew for the first time with absolute clarity that it was only the faith that the blind man returned his love and had forgiven him which had made it possible for him to bear their misery so patiently. He could not give up this hope all of a sudden. He felt that his brother was just as necessary to him as he was to his brother. He could not and did not want to desert him. He either had to bear his

mistrust, or find some way to convince the
blind man of the groundlessness of his suspicion.
Oh, if only in some way he could secure a
gold piece! If to-morrow morning he could
only say to the blind man, "I only put it away,
so you wouldn't spend it for drink with the
laborers, so that people wouldn't steal it from
you" . . . or something like that.

Steps were approaching on the wooden stair;
the travelers were going to bed. Suddenly an
idea flashed through his head; to knock at the
door opposite, to tell the strangers the whole
truth of what had happened to-day, and to ask
them for twenty francs. But he immediately
realized that this was entirely useless! They
would not even believe his story. And now he
remembered how the pale one had started with
fright when he, Carlo, had suddenly appeared
out of the darkness in front of the carriage.

He stretched out on the straw mattress. It
was absolutely dark in the room. Now he heard
the laborers talking loudly and going with
heavy steps down the wooden stairs. A little
later both the gates were locked. Once more
the hostler went up and down the stairs, then
everything was silent. All that Carlo heard
now was Geronimo's snoring. Soon his

thoughts fell into confusion with the begin-
nings of dreams. When he awoke, deep darkness was still about him. He looked toward the
spot where the window was; when he strained
his eye he recognized there in the centre of the
impenetrable blackness, a deep-gray quad-
rangle.

Geronimo still slept the heavy sleep of a
drunken man. And Carlo thought of the day
which the morrow was. It made him shudder.
He thought of the night after this day, of the
day after this night, of the future which lay
ahead of him; dread of the loneliness which
was before him filled him. Why had he not
been more courageous in the evening? Why
had he not approached the strangers, and
asked them for twenty francs? Perhaps they
would have had pity on him. And yet—
perhaps it was well he had not asked them.
And why was it well? . . . He sat up suddenly,
and felt his heart beating. He knew why it
was well. If they had refused him, he would
nevertheless have remained under suspicion—
but now. . . . He stared at the gray spot, which
began to grow a little lighter. . . . That which
involuntarily had run through his mind was
impossible, entirely impossible! . . . The door

across the way was shut—and besides, they might wake up. . . . Yes, there—the gray luminous spot in the centre of the darkness was the new day.

Carlo got up, as if something were drawing him thither, and touched the cold pane with his forehead. Why had he gotten up? . . . To make the attempt? . . . But why? . . . It was impossible—and besides it was a crime. A crime? What could twenty francs mean to people like them who travel thousands of miles for pleasure? They would not even notice that they were missing. . . . He went to the door, and opened it softly. The other one was opposite, locked; it was only two steps away. On a nail in the door-post their clothes were hanging. Carlo felt them with his hand. . . .

Yes, if people left their purses in their pockets, life would be very simple indeed, for then soon no one would have to go begging. . . . But the pockets were empty. What was there to do now? Back to the room, to the straw mattress. Perhaps there was a better way yet to secure the twenty francs—one less dangerous and more honored. If he actually always held back several centisimi from the alms until he had saved up twenty francs, and then bought

the gold piece. . . . But how long might that
take—months, perhaps a year. Oh, if he only
had the courage! He was still standing in the
hall. He looked over at the door. . . . What
sort of streak was this that fell on the floor
vertically from the top? Was it possible? The
door was left ajar, not locked? . . . Why was
he surprised at this? For months past it had
been impossible to lock the door. What for?
He remembered; people had slept here only
three times this summer; twice, journeymen,
and once a tourist who had hurt his foot. The
door would not lock—all he needed now was
courage—yes, and luck! Courage?

The worst that could happen to him was
that the two would wake, and even then he
could still find an excuse. He peered through
the crack into the room. It was still so dark
that he could only recognize the outlines of the
two figures lying on the beds. He listened;
they were breathing quietly and evenly. Carlo
gently opened the door, and on his bare feet
entered the room noiselessly. The two beds
were arranged lengthwise along the same wall,
opposite the window. In the centre of the
room stood a table. Carlo stole up to it. He
ran with his hand across the top, and felt a

bunch of keys, a penknife, a little book—
nothing else . . . why, of course? . . . Absurd,
that he should have imagined they would place
their money on the table! It would be best to
get right out now. . . . And yet, perhaps it
would take no more than a good grasp, and
luck would be with him. . . . And he approached
closer to the bed by the door; something lay on
the chair—he felt for it—it was a revolver.
Carlo started. . . . Had he not better take it
and keep it? Why has this man a revolver
lying ready? If he should awake, and see
him. . . . But no, he would say, "It is three
o'clock, sir, time to get up! . . ." And he left
the revolver where it was.

And he stole further into the room. Here on
the other chair, among articles of apparel. . . .
Dear heavens! There it was . . . a purse—
He held it in his hand! . . . At the same moment he heard a slight creaking. With a quick
movement he stretched down full length at the
foot of the bed. . . . Again the creaking—a
deep breathing—a clearing of the throat—
then all was silent, profoundly silent. Carlo
remained lying on the floor, the purse in his
hand, waiting. Nothing stirred any longer.
Dawn already fell palely into the room. Carlo

did not dare rise, but crawled on the floor
toward the door. It was wide enough open to
let him through; he continued crawling until
he was out in the hall, and only then did he
slowly rise, with a deep breath.

He opened the purse; it was divided into
three parts; on the right and left only small
pieces of silver. Carlo now opened the middle
compartment, which was shut by an additional
clasp, and felt three twenty-franc pieces. For
a moment he considered taking two of them,
but he quickly put aside this temptation; he
took out only one gold piece, and closed the
purse again. Then he kneeled down, and
looked through the crack into the room, where
everything was perfectly still again, and he
gave the purse a push, so that it slid down
under the second bed.

When the stranger woke up he would assume
that it had fallen from the chair. Carlo got up
slowly. The floor creaked slightly, and at the
same moment he heard a voice from within,
"Hello? What's the matter?" Carlo quickly
retreated two steps, holding his breath, and
slipped into his room. He was safe, and listened. . . . The bed across the way creaked
again, and then all was silent. He held the

gold piece between his fingers. He had succeeded—succeeded! He had the twenty francs,
and now he could say to his brother, "You see
that I am not a thief!" And to-day they would
take up their wanderings again toward the
south, to Bormio, then further through the
Valtellina . . . then to Tirano. . .to Edole. . .to
Breno . . . to Lake Iseo, as last year. . . . There
would be nothing to arouse suspicion, because
only the day before yesterday he had said to
the innkeeper, "In a couple of days we'll be
going down."

It grew lighter, the entire room lay in a gray
dawn. Ah, if Geronimo would only soon wake
up! It is pleasant to walk early in the morning!
They will start before sunrise. A good-morning
to the innkeeper, the hostler, and Maria, and
then away, away. . . .   Not until they have
walked two hours, and are already near the
valley, would he tell Geronimo.

Geronimo turned and stretched himself.
Carlo called to him, "Geronimo!"

"Well, what do you want?" And he supported himself on both his hands, and sat up.

"Geronimo, let us get up."

"What for?" And he turned his dead eyes
toward his brother. Carlo knew that he was

now remembering yesterday's incident, and he
knew also that he would not say another word
about it until he was drunk again.

"It is cold, Geronimo, let us go. Things
won't improve this season; I think we had
better go. By noon we will be in Boladore."

Geronimo rose. The noises of the awakening
house were becoming audible. Down in the
courtyard the innkeeper was talking with the
hostler. Carlo got up, and went down. He
was always up early, and often in the half-
light of dawn went out to the road. He went
up to the innkeeper, and said, "We are going
to leave."

"Ah, so soon?" asked the innkeeper.

"Yes. It's too cold already when we stand
here in the yard, and the wind goes hard."

"Well, remember me to Baldetti, when you
get to Bormio, and tell him he isn't to forget to
send me the oil."

"Yes, I'll do that. Besides—today's lodg-
ing?"

He fumbled in his bag.

"Never mind, Carlo," said the innkeeper.
"I'll make a present of the twenty centisimi;
I listened to his singing too. Good morning."

"Thank you," said Carlo. "Besides, we are

not in such a hurry. We'll see you again, when
you come back from the shacks; Bormio won't
move from where it is, will it?" He laughed,
and went up the wooden stairs.

Geronimo stood in the middle of the room,
and said, "Well, I am ready to leave."

"Right away," said Carlo.

Out of an old bureau, which stood in a corner
of the room, he took their few belongings, and
tied them up in a bundle. Then he said, "A
fine day, but very cold."

"I know," said Geronimo. Both left the
room.

"Walk softly," said Carlo; "the two that
arrived last night are sleeping here." Stepping
carefully, they went downstairs.

"The innkeeper wants to be remembered
to you," said Carlo; "he made us a present of
the twenty centisimi for last night. He is down
at the shacks, and won't be back for two hours.
Anyhow, we'll see him again next year."

Geronimo did not reply. They went out on
the highway which lay before them in the faint
light of dawn. Carlo took hold of his brother's
left arm, and together they walked in silence
down toward the valley. After a short stretch
they reached the spot where the road began to

run in long windings. Mists were climbing
upward, toward them, and the heights above
them seemed as if ensnared by the clouds.
And Carlo thought, Now I will tell him.

Carlo, however, said not a word, but took
the gold piece out of his pocket, and handed it
to his brother, who took it with the fingers of
his right hand. Then he carried it to his cheek
and forehead, and finally he nodded. "I knew
it," he said.

"And yes," replied Carlo, looking at Geronimo in an estranged way.

"Even if the stranger hadn't told me, I
would have known."

"And yes," said Carlo helplessly. "But you
understand why up there, before all the others
—I was afraid—that you would all at once—
—And see, Geronimo, thought I to myself,
that it was about time you bought a new coat
and a shirt and shoes; I thought; that is
why . . ."

The blind man shook his head violently.
"Why?" And with one hand he felt along his
coat. "Good enough, warm enough; we are
now going south."

Carlo didn't understand it. Geronimo didn't
seem glad, he didn't make excuses. And he

went on talking, "Geronimo, didn't I do right? Aren't you glad? Now we've got it anyhow, haven't we? Now we have all of it. If I had told you up there, who knows. . . . Oh, it is good I didn't tell you—yes, surely."

Then Geronimo screamed, "Stop your lying, Carlo; I am sick of it!"

Carlo stood still, and let go of his brother's arm. "I am not lying."

"But I know you are lying! You are lying all the time! You've lied a hundred times already! You wanted to keep this for yourself too, but you were afraid, that's all!"

Carlo bowed his head, and did not reply. He again took hold of the blind man's arm, and went on with him. It hurt him that Geronimo spoke thus; but he was really surprised that he wasn't sadder yet.

The fogs parted. After a long silence, Geronimo said, "It is getting warm." He said it indifferently, as if it were something obvious, as he had said it hundreds of times, and at this same moment Carlo felt, "Nothing had changed as far as Geronimo was concerned. For him he had always been a thief."

"Are you hungry?" he asked.

Geronimo nodded, and took a piece of cheese

and bread out of his coat pocket and ate of it. And they went on.

The mail from Bormio passed them. The driver called to them, "Going down already?" Then other carriages came, all going upward.

"Wind from the valley," said Geronimo, and, after a sharp turn, the Valtellina lay at their feet.

Truly—nothing had changed, thought Carlo. Now I have stolen on his account—and it has all been useless.

The fog below them thinned out more and more; the gleam of the sun tore holes into it. And Carlo thought, "Perhaps it wasn't wise after all to leave the inn so soon. The purse is lying under the bed; no doubt that looks suspicious . . . " But how immaterial it all seemed! What dreadful thing could still happen to him? His brother, the light of whose eyes he had destroyed, believed he was robbed by him, had believed it for years, and would always believe it. What more dreadful thing was there that could happen to him?

Below them lay the great white hotel, immersed in the morning's glow, and further down, where the valley began to widen, the

village stretched out. Silently the two continued their way, and Carlo's hand lay always
on the blind man's arm. They went past the
grounds of the hotel, and on the terrace Carlo
saw guests in light summer clothes, sitting at
breakfast.

"Where do you want to stay?" asked Carlo.

"At the 'Eagle,' as always."

When they had come to the little inn at the
end of the village, they entered. They sat
down, and ordered wine.

"What are you doing down here so early?"
asked the proprietor.

Carlo was a little startled at the question.
"Is it so early? The tenth or eleventh of Sep-
tember—isn't it?"

"Last year it certainly was much later when
you came down."

"It's already cold up there," said Carlo.
"We nearly froze last night. And yes, I was to
remind you not to forget to send up the oil."

The air in the inn was heavy and thick. A
strange restlessness fell upon Carlo; he wanted
to be out in the open air again, on the great
highway, that led to Tirano, to Edole, to Lake

Iseo, everywhere into the distance! Suddenly
he got up.

"Are we leaving already?" asked Geronimo.

"Didn't we intend to be in Boladore by noon?
The carriages stop at the 'Stag' for their mid-
day rest; it is a good place."

And they went. Benozzi, the barber, stood
smoking in front of his shop. "Good morning," he called to them. "How does it look up
there? Suppose it snowed last night?"

"Yes, yes," said Carlo, and hastened his
steps.

The village lay behind them; the road wound
white among the meadows and vineyards along
the noisy river. The sky was blue and silent.
"Why did I do it?" thought Carlo. He looked
sideways at the blind man. "Does his face
look different from other times? He always
believed it—I've always been alone—and he
has always hated me." And it seemed to him
as if he were walking onward under a heavy
load, which he never could throw off his shoulders; it seemed as if he could see the night
through which Geronimo walked by his side,
while the gleaming sun lay on all the roads.

And they went on, went and went for hours.

From time to time Geronimo sat down on a milestone, or the two of them leaned against the railing of a bridge in order to rest. Again they passed through a village. In front of the inn stood carriages, travelers had gotten out and walked to and fro; but the two beggars did not halt. Out again upon the open road. The sun rose higher; it must be near noon. It was a day like a thousand others.

"The tower of Boladore," said Geronimo. Carlo looked up. He was surprised how accurately Geronimo was able to reckon distances. The tower of Boladore really did appear on the horizon. At a considerable distance some one was coming toward them. It seemed to Carlo as if he had been sitting along the roadside, and had suddenly gotten up. The figure came closer. Now Carlo saw that it was a gendarme, one of those they so often met on the road. Yet Carlo started slightly. But when the man came closer, Carlo recognized him, and was reassured. It was Pietro Tenelli. Only in May had the two beggars sat with him in Raggazzi's inn at Morignone, and he had told them a terrible tale of how he had once almost been stabbed to death by a vagabond.

"Some one has stopped," said Geronimo.

"Tenelli, the gendarme," said Carlo.

By now they had come up to him.

"Good morning, Signor Tenelli," said Carlo, and remained standing in front of him.

"It happens," said the gendarme, "that I have to take both of you to headquarters at Boladore."

"Eh?" cried the blind man.

Carlo turned pale. "How is that possible?" he thought. "It can't be on that account. They can't know about it down here already."

"It seems to be the way you are going," said the gendarme, laughing, "and I don't suppose it makes any difference if we go together."

"Why don't you say something, Carlo?" asked Geronimo.

"Oh yes, I'll talk. . . . Please, Signor Gendarme, how is it possible . . . what have we . . . or rather, what have I . . . really, I don't know . . . ."

"Well, it just happens. Maybe you are innocent. How do I know? Anyhow, we got a telegram at headquarters to stop you, because you are suspected, very much suspected, of having stolen money from people up there.

Well, it may be you are innocent. Now, move on!"

"Why don't you say something, Carlo?" asked Geronimo.

"I'll talk—oh yes, I'll talk."

"Now move on! What sense is there in standing here on the road? The sun burns like fire. In an hour we'll be there. Move on!"

Carlo, as always, touched Geronimo's arm, and so they slowly went on, the gendarme following them.

"Carlo, why don't you say something?" Geronimo asked again.

"What do you want, Geronimo, what am I to say? It will all clear up; I don't know myself . . ."

And the thought flashed through his head, Shall I explain it to him, before we appear at court? I don't suppose I had better. The gendarme will hear us. Well, what does it matter? I'll tell the truth anyhow in court. "Your honor," I will say, "this isn't a theft like the usual one. It happened in this way . . ." And he struggled to find the words to explain the circumstance clearly and intelligibly to the court: "A man drove through the pass yesterday . . . he may have been a crazy man — or maybe he was only mistaken . . . and this man . . ."

But what nonsense! Who would believe it? No one would believe this ridiculous story. Not even Geronimo believes it. And he looked at him from one side. According to its old habit, the head of the blind man moved up and down as if keeping time to his walk, but the face was motionless and the vacant eyes stared into the air. And Carlo knew suddenly what thoughts were running behind his forehead. "So that's the way things are," Geronimo no doubt thought. "Carlo not only steals from me, but he robs other people too. Well, it's easy for him, he has eyes that can see, and he uses them . . ." That is what Geronimo was thinking, no doubt. And even the fact that no money can be found on me won't help me—neither with the judge, nor with Geronimo. They will lock me up, and him. Yes, him as well as me, for he has the piece of money.

And he could not think beyond this, his mind was too confused. It seemed to him as if he no longer understood anything of the entire circumstance. He knew only one thing: he would gladly go to prison for a year . . . or for ten, if only Geronimo would come to realize that it was for his sake alone he had become a thief.

And suddenly Geronimo stood still, so that Carlo too had to halt.

"Well, what's the trouble?" said the gendarme angrily. "Move on, move on!" But in surprise he saw that the blind man had let his guitar fall to the ground, raised his arms, and felt with both hands for his brother's cheeks. Then he brought his lips close to Carlo's mouth, who at first did not know what was happening to him, and kissed him.

"Are you crazy?" asked the gendarme. "Move on, move on! I have no mind roasting here!"

Geronimo picked his guitar from the ground without saying a word. Carlo took a deep breath, and again put his hand on the blind man's arm. Was it possible? His brother was no longer angry with him? Perhaps he understood at last—? And he looked at him doubtfully from the side.

"Move on!" growled the gendarme. "Get going—" and he gave Carlo a punch in the ribs.

And Carlo, leading the arm of the blind man with a firm grip, went onward again. He hit

a much faster pace than before. He saw Geronimo smile in a mild, perfectly happy fashion,
such as he had not seen since his childhood
days. And Carlo smiled too. It seemed as if
nothing terrible could happen to him now—
neither at court, nor anywhere else in the
world. He had found his brother again . . .
No, he was really his own for the first time.

THE END